MEN OF INKED: SOUTHSIDE

Flow
Men of Inked: Southside

by
Chelle Bliss

COPYRIGHT

Flow @ Bliss Ink LLC

Published by Bliss Ink & Chelle Bliss
Published on October 2nd 2018
Edited by Silently Correcting Your Grammar
Proofread by Julie Deaton & Rosa Sharon
Cover Photo © Wander Aguilar
Cover Design © Lori Jackson Design

Grandma,
I've been blessed to have you in my life. I won the
lottery the day I was born into this fun, crazy, and
sometimes loud Italian family.

Thank you for making me always feel loved and being
the best grandma in the world.

Chelle

CHAPTER ONE

DAPHNE

I DIDN'T THINK I'd feel this way. Laying eyes on my father after years of him being in prison is kind of like seeing someone rise from their grave.

He's aged a bit since the last time I visited him. Two years into his sentence, he denied any further visitors, including my mom, which didn't sit well with anyone in the family, but most of all her.

I suppose spending years behind bars can age a person prematurely, even someone as strong and stubborn as my father. From everything I know about prison life, nothing is easy, and the evidence is written all over my father's face. The lines around his eyes, which used to be faint and barely visible, are deep and stark against his olive skin. His black hair has larger swaths of white, mostly framing his handsome face.

Ma's the first one to make her way to him, throwing her arms around his shoulders as soon as she's close enough. My father holds her tight, tucking his face into the crook of her neck as he lifts her off the floor and spins her in the air.

They've been through this before. My dad has spent most of my life in and out of prison, never learning his lesson.

There's a brief moment of hope as I watch them embrace, hoping he's *reformed* after this last stint. But then again, he's Santino Gallo, and he's never seemed to learn.

They say you can't teach an old dog new tricks, but I disagree. My father learned; he just ignored the hell out of the lessons, preferring to live life on his own terms, always bucking the system.

Lucky us.

At first, no one seems to notice my father's presence besides my mother and me. But then, just like something out of a movie, the music stops playing, and the entire room goes silent. All eyes are on my parents, watching as they embrace.

I lift the whiskey to my lips, taking another sip as I try to collect my thoughts. The moment should be a happy occasion, but part of me is pissed. This is Lucio and Delilah's day, not my dad's, but he always finds a way to make everything about him.

"Well." Angelo comes up behind me and places his hands on the bar. "This should be interesting."

"One word for you." I set down my empty glass and turn to face him. "Clusterfuck."

"Maybe he won't be so bad this time," he tells me, and we both start laughing.

We know the thought is utter nonsense.

We know Santino.

We know his tricks.

His lies.

At my father's core is a good man. A loving father and mostly, at least the last time he was out, a faithful and caring partner.

"Pop's back," Vinnie tells us like the entire wedding reception isn't seeing him with our very own eyes.

"Way to go, Captain Obvious," Angelo teases.

Vinnie has had the least amount of time with my father. Being the youngest, most of his life my dad was in prison. Even with that, Vinnie still idolized my father and always thought the best of him. We knew better. Years of disappointment will do that to people.

If it weren't for Angelo and Lucio, I don't know where Vinnie would be. They made him the man he is today, giving him guidance and advice as he navigated his teen years.

"He has the oddest timing. Why can't he ever be

normal?" I ask as I shake my head. "The man has no limits or shame."

"Shit's about to get sideways," Lucio says as he comes to stand near the three of us, with Delilah at his side.

"Aren't you guys happy?" Delilah glances between us. She doesn't know the complexity of my father and the years of his bullshit either.

"Of course we are. He's our dad, but he doesn't make life easy for anyone." Lucio pulls her tighter to his side and kisses her head. "You'll learn soon enough."

"He can't be any worse than my father," Delilah says, putting things into perspective for all of us.

Delilah knows all about messed-up fathers. I'd rather deal with my dad's revolving door at the local prison than her father's alcoholic tantrums.

Even after months apart, her father hasn't bothered to contact her. He really just washed his hands of her, preferring to pretend she never existed than to clean up his act and beg for her forgiveness. At least my dad never did anything to hurt me. He may have been a selfish prick at times, but he never did us any long-lasting harm.

"My *bambini*," my father says as he walks toward us with his arms outstretched like a proud papa and not an ex-con.

He's wearing a new suit, no doubt having planned to make his grand entrance during the wedding without clueing the rest of us in on his release date.

My mother's behind him, glaring at us. We aren't running into our father's waiting arms like she did, and she's not too happy. I love my mother. There's no other person on the planet I adore more than her, but man, she doesn't seem to have a grip or any willpower when it comes to my dad.

I turn around, glancing over at Lucio and pretending my mother isn't giving us the evil eye. "Is he serious?"

Lucio doesn't answer back. Just shakes his head, at a loss for words.

Papa clearly didn't get the memo about our not being overly thrilled about his return. The fact that our mother is asking for us to hire him on at Hook & Hustle —which means telling us, because there's no saying no to Betty—just adds another layer of complication. It sure as hell doesn't help in the feelings department either.

Vinnie's the first one to grab my dad, almost lifting him off the floor in a giant bear hug. "We missed you," he tells him, like he's speaking for all of us.

Which he's not.

I remember a time when I felt like Vinnie. But after the third, or maybe it was the fourth, time we went through the prison release celebration bullshit, I became jaded.

Who wouldn't be?

Saying goodbye to my father over and over again because he can't follow the law gets tiring after a while. When all my friends' dads were attending Father-Daughter dances at school, I had one of my big brothers at my side because my dad was doing hard time for some stupid shit he easily could've avoided. But he always chose crime over his family.

"Jesus," Papa says to Vinnie as soon as his feet touch the floor again. He gazes up at his youngest son and grabs him by the shoulder, squeezing his muscles. "You've grown." My father practically beams with pride.

There's a smart comment on the tip of my tongue about missing Vinnie's last growth spurt. Angelo elbows me, knowing I am about to open my big mouth and probably say something I'll later regret.

Vinnie was in high school when my father last got popped and sentenced to seven years hard time. Papa missed so many milestones. He wasn't there when Vinnie won the state championship or became Illinois Quarterback of the Year during his senior year. Both of which were things we celebrated as a family, minus my dad.

While my dad was away, Vinnie had a big growth spurt, adding a good six inches to his then-already six-foot frame. He's a monster. Wide. Muscular. And everything a star football player should be.

"He's a big boy," Ma says. "Wait until you see him play."

My papa's staring at Vinnie with wide eyes. Maybe surprised at his size or sad at everything he's missed. The reality of the time he'll never get back has to hit him square in the face when seeing a full-grown man standing in front of him, instead of the teenage boy he left behind.

"I'll be at every game," my father promises.

It's hard for me not to roll my eyes. This happens every time he gets out of the joint. He's full of promises. He means well and probably thinks he'll follow through, but he's always pulled back into the criminal world and away from us.

Lucio leans forward and whispers, "Are we doing an over-under this time?"

The last two times he came out of prison a changed man, we bet on how long it would be before he ended up behind bars again. This time won't be any different. So far, Angelo's two for two, always nailing the exact amount of time before my father is arrested again.

"Years or months?" Angelo asks in a hushed tone.

"Years may be too optimistic," I tell them. "I give him six months."

"I say a year," Lucio replies.

"Nine months, tops," Angelo adds.

I'm not the only jaded Gallo kid. We know my father all too well and aren't fooled by his false promises anymore. Vinnie, though, he's still too innocent and hopeful to let our sourness seep into his system.

7

My father closes the space between us, arms outstretched like we're having a grand homecoming and couldn't wait to see him again.

I used to be a daddy's girl a long time ago. There was a time when I'd leap into his arms and squeal with delight. She's gone now, but the reality hasn't quite caught up with my father.

"Look at my kids. So grown. So beautiful," he says.

"Dad." There's no warmth in Angelo's voice.

"Pop." Lucio nods.

"Hey, Papa," I say because I've never called him anything else to his face. "You look well."

"Daphne, you've turned into a magnificent creature."

"It wasn't overnight," I blurt out, getting in a small dig about how long he's been gone.

He shakes his head, knowing he's fucked up. "It won't happen again. I'll never go back there. I swear."

My ma's practically hanging on him, happier than all of us to have her man back at her side. She's always been a sucker for my dad. I don't know of another woman on the planet who would put up with his bull-shit, but she does somehow.

"This is your new daughter-in-law, Delilah." Ma dips her head toward Dee.

"You're more beautiful than the photos," my father says.

"It's nice to finally meet you," Delilah replies and

runs her hand down the front of her gown, smoothing out the material.

She looks absolutely stunning today. Don't get me wrong, Delilah is always beautiful. But there's something about a bride on her wedding day that'll always knock everyone's socks off.

Lucio and Angelo have their arms crossed, looking like bouncers at a swanky club in their polished suits and big muscles, with absolutely no smiles.

"Don't be that way," my father says and waves his hand in the air. He steps forward and throws his arms around my older brothers at the same time, hugging them. "I'm home now. Don't worry about anything. I have everything covered."

Those are the words we most fear. My dad's idea of having everything covered always involves shady shit and a trip to the police precinct.

"Let's get this party started," my father says, pointing toward the DJ. My father takes my mother under his arm and wraps the other arm around Lucio. "Let's celebrate. This is a big day."

Lucio doesn't even grumble. Maybe the happiness of the day is too big to let my father's presence cast a shadow over everything. The wedding guests start to chatter again as the shock of my father's presence starts to wear off.

"I'm changing my bet to three months," Angelo tells me as we watch them saunter up to the bar. "He hasn't changed a bit."

_v_ Angelo's right.

ino Gallo's the same proud, charismatic, law-
man he was five years ago when he was
arrested. How he convinced the parole board to let him
out nearly two years early, I'll never understand. I'm
sure he charmed them with his promises of being a
changed man. Hopefully this time, he doesn't land on
every television news station in the city for whatever
crap he pulls because he can't seem to fit into society
and be normal.

I crave normal.

I want simple.

But somehow, I never seem to take the easy road...a
trait I clearly inherited from my parents.

No one says anything as my father hands out
glasses of champagne. We're all staring at each other,
trying to pretend we're happy to have him back. We
know our mother expects us to act like we're excited,
but it's not so easy to pull off. Deep down, we are
happy to have him home and safe. How could we not
feel that way? He's our father, after all. But that doesn't
mean there isn't hurt and anger there too.

"To Lucio, Delilah, and new beginnings." Papa lifts
his glass, waiting for each of us to do the same.

"Cincin," my brothers say in unison, finally caving
when my mother's eyes narrow.

I chug the champagne, wishing I were buzzed
already. Alcohol always seems to make awkward situations like this a little easier to swallow. Right now, I

could use a little liquid courage, or as I like to call it, liquid amnesia.

"Santino." Uncle Sal's voice is unmistakable as he comes up behind me.

I turn toward my uncle with the champagne flute still against my lips and lift my eyebrows. I know this is about to get good.

Salvatore Gallo has very little patience for his brother...my father. They are complete opposites except for their faces. If I didn't know better, I'd think they were twins with their salt-and-pepper hair and devilish good looks. But everything else about them is totally different. Uncle Sal is a dedicated family man, where my father cares more about his *business*.

There was bad blood for years. They didn't speak after a falling-out. Tempers have cooled over time, maybe because they're getting older.

Just before my father went back to prison, they had made amends and put the past behind them. But then things changed, and the Gallo name was dragged through the mud, chilling the relationship again. But my uncle Sal didn't let that affect how he treated the rest of us. He knew we were nothing like our father.

"Sal." My father's smiling from ear to ear. "I've missed you, brother."

Somehow, I avoid spitting my mouthful of champagne all over everyone at my father's bald-faced lie.

"You've always had great timing," Uncle Sal says, and his voice is oozing attitude. Standing behind Sal are his children—Joseph, Michael, Anthony, Thomas, and Izzy—waiting for fireworks just like I am.

My father has always called his brother Sal "elitist." He thinks Sal not only snubbed his nose at his roots, but the entire family, when he moved away to Tampa. He did, but not because he was too good for us. My dad was the biggest problem, and the pressure pushing down on Uncle Sal by association was tremendous.

I don't blame him for leaving. I probably would've too if I could have. For years, I thought about changing my name, but I knew it wouldn't help. In my neighborhood, everyone knew my father and our illustrious past, so there was no reason to go through the hassle.

I like my uncle Sal and my cousins too. I only wished they'd stuck around a little longer and been part of my life instead of setting off for the warm sand of Florida when I was young.

My father's attention doesn't linger too long on his brother before turning to Aunt Maria, Sal's wife. "Mar, you're looking better than ever." Papa winks at her in a playful way. No doubt trying to piss off his brother.

"Tino," Aunt Maria says at her husband's side, but she's not amused or feeling the same playfulness as my dad.

The funny thing is, Aunt Mar is so much like my mother, it's not even funny. They look entirely different, but goddamn, they're both bossy and nosy as hell.

My father's sister looks him up and down. "Hello,

Santino." Aunt Fran crosses her arms in front of her chest. "You're looking..." Her voice trails off and her top lip curls.

Her husband, Bear, wraps his arm around her waist like he's trying to hold her back and whispers something in her ear.

In the short amount of time I've spent with Bear, I've found him oddly fascinating. Looking at him, you'd think he'd be all badass, but he's just a giant teddy bear —and a complete pervert too. He has my aunt Fran all tied up in knots, which is something I thought I'd never see again.

After a bad breakup with her first husband, I never thought she'd fall in love again. She was way too fond of track suits and tennis shoes to get much more than a sideways glance from another man. But now, she's like a different person, showing more skin than I'd ever seen her do before.

"Fran, you're a sight for sore eyes." Papa doesn't dare try to touch her.

No other woman, besides my mother, scares the crap out of him quite like his sister. She's a tiny thing, but man, the mouth on her gives me life goals.

"I need a drink," Fran says, glancing over her shoulder at her silver fox husband. "Something stiff."

Bear smirks, brushing his lips against her cheek. "Baby, I got..."

"Don't say it," Fran warns as her top lip flattens.

"What's your poison, Aunt Fran?" I ask.

I want nothing more than to drown the insanity that is my family in the bottom of a few shots of whatever she thinks is stiff.

"Whiskey, baby." She smiles.

"I like it when you drink tequila," Bear whines.

I bite back my laughter. If she's anything like me, I lose all common sense and control when I've had even a moderate amount of tequila. It's not pretty, and I am never proud of the way I behave after I've spent the night with Mr. Cuervo.

"That's why I want whiskey," she tells him and cocks an eyebrow, but he doesn't argue.

"I'll grab a few bottles." I place my empty glass on the bar, ready to go back to the harder stuff.

"My kinda girl," Bear says with a wink.

Izzy, my cousin and Uncle Sal's only daughter, catches up with me as I walk to the other end of the bar, needing a break from my family.

"You okay?" She touches my arm as I lean over the bar and realize my tits are almost spilling out of my dress.

"I'm great. Just fucking peachy." I adjust my strapless bra which is digging into my skin and silently curse Delilah for her ugly-ass choices in dresses.

"I'm here if you want to talk," Izzy says.

My cousin is nothing short of perfect. Her skin is flawless, her hair is spot-on, and her outfit is to die for. But all my cousins are perfect, especially Sal's kids.

Meanwhile, I'm in a hideous strapless chiffon

nightmare with so many ruffles on the front, I might as well not have tits because no one can see through the layers anyway.

"Thanks, Izzy. I'd rather not talk about him. Let's talk about you instead. I've heard some pretty interesting rumors."

"Rumors?" She raises her perfectly shaped brown eyebrow and smirks. "Like, what kind of rumors?"

"I hear you have quite the man on your hands. I don't know how you do it. I mean, if some guy bossed me around, I'd probably knee him square in his junk."

I keep my response tame so as not to hurt her feelings. I don't know how much she wants to share, and honestly, what she does in the bedroom is none of my damn business.

Izzy laughs, covering her lipstick-stained mouth with her hand. "It's not what you think."

"He doesn't boss you around and tell you what to do?"

She waves me off. "Only in the bedroom. But everywhere else, I'm the boss."

The bartender walks over and glances at us, perking up a little even though he's got one foot in the grave. "What can I get you, ladies?"

"Three bottles of whiskey. Top-shelf."

"Three?" He leans forward like he didn't quite hear me right. "You sure?"

I nod and hold up three fingers. "Three."

"It'll be a moment," he says before disappearing.

"A man better give me a whole lot of pleasure for him to tell me what to do in the sack."

"He does." She's beaming, and part of me hates her just a little bit more. "And it's not as bad as you think."

It's my turn to raise my eyebrows and stare. "I can't wrap my head around it."

"You haven't known pleasure until you completely surrender. You should try it sometime."

I want to tell her to fuck off, but I can't. She looks entirely too happy, and her husband is a fine specimen of a man. He could probably make me drop to my knees and beg for an ass-whoopin' too. He's that good-looking. They make a perfect couple with all their perfectness.

It's irritating.

"Here you go," the bartender says, saving me from saying something I'm almost sure I'll totally regret.

"Ready?" I ask her, grabbing the bottles, and dip my head toward the two stacks of glasses the bartender slides across the bar.

She scoops the glasses into her arms and follows me toward the tables where my cousins have already made themselves comfortable.

Our parents aren't there. They're on the dance floor, putting Fred and Ginger to shame.

"We're not waiting for them," Morgan, Fran's son, says as he grabs a bottle as soon as I set the whiskey down on the table.

"Never thought I'd see the day when they'd all be

in the same room again." Joe, my cousin, ticks his chin toward the dance floor as he kicks back and takes the glass of whiskey Morgan hands to him. Suzy, Joe's wife, is at his side, curling into her husband but not drinking.

"It's crazy." Michael, Joe's brother, leans back and shakes his head.

I stare at my cousins, wondering what life must have been like for them. Here, there's only us, but there in Florida, they have each other. We used to have Morgan, but that was before my cousins lured him away from us with promises of warm winters and an amazing job.

I hate them all just a little. I shouldn't, though, because they're family. But it's hard not to feel that way. They're all happy and tanned, not looking as pale or miserable as my brothers and me.

"It's weird, right?" Morgan holds a glass in front of his lips and pauses. "But the night's early. There's plenty of time for bloodshed."

CHAPTER TWO

DAPHNE

MY LEGS WOBBLE as I stagger away from the dessert table after consuming more cake than should be allowed for one human being. Walking gracefully is damn near impossible after the amount of whiskey I've already consumed and the ridiculously high heels Delilah made me wear.

I'm making my way through the sea of wedding guests, concentrating a little too hard on each step, when my heel catches. I start to tumble forward and let out a loud screech, knowing I'm about to face-plant onto the dance floor in front of everybody.

My arms flail around, and I'm cursing whiskey for making this all possible as I fall forward. Just as I brace myself for impact, trying to avoid smashing my face, strong arms wrap around my waist and haul me backward.

I blink a few times, staring at the dark green carpet a few feet in front of me where I was no doubt going to land with my dress flipped over my head, letting everyone know I didn't bother with underwear.

My heart's pounding as my back collides with a warm body, and I gasp. "Easy there." The man holds me tightly, saving me from what would've been one of the most embarrassing moments of my life. His voice is so deep, my skin prickles the moment he whispers in my ear.

"Shit." I grab my chest, trying to calm myself after my near-death experience. Okay. Maybe I'm being overdramatic, but at the very least, falling on the ballroom floor in front of the three hundred guests is something I never would've lived down.

"I got you," he says, and this time, the deep honey sound of his voice sends goose bumps streaming down my skin as if a line of dominoes has been tipped over.

His arm is around me, hand gripping my hip on one side, holding me so damn tight I can barely breathe. I turn, glancing over my shoulder at my savior, wondering who the mystery man is, and praying like hell he isn't a cousin.

That would be awkward.

But instead, I'm met by a pair of honey-brown eyes the color of sin and everything unholy. We're face-to-face, his front to my back and his arm still holding me close.

My mouth moves, but nothing comes out. I'm too lost in the way his eyes seem to pierce my soul.

"Are you okay?" the dreamboat asks.

I gawk at him and do nothing to put space between us. All I can do is nod. I don't trust myself to speak without sounding like a prepubescent schoolgirl, and I sure as hell can't seem to walk without totally embarrassing myself either.

His cheeks rise, almost touching the bottom of his eyes, as he stares at me...laughing. Every ounce of mortification I may have felt vanishes instantly, and the dreamboat doesn't seem as hot anymore.

"You can get your hands off me now," I tell him as I narrow my eyes.

How dare he laugh at me. You can't save someone and then laugh in her face at the hilarity of the entire situation.

"Don't be that way," he tells me, as if I'm being completely unreasonable, which I'm not.

"I'm not being any way. Thanks for the save, but you can let go of me now." My teeth grind together, and my body goes rigid.

He tightens his hold and puts his mouth near my ear. "*Bella,*" he whispers. "Maybe I like the way you feel against me."

21

My body betrays me as I practically shudder in his arms because, damn it, I like the way I feel in his arms too.

The deep musk of his cologne permeates the air around us, filling my senses with everything dreamboat. His thumb strokes just below my rib, slowly moving up and down, doing nothing to make pulling away from him any easier.

"Want to get out of here and find someplace quiet to talk?" he asks.

I turn my face toward him again, bringing our lips so close we're almost kissing. I want to ask him if that line works for him, but I don't. There's no doubt in my mind his words sure as hell do work for him.

The whiskey doesn't help me make a rational decision. I should say no. I know that. I should tell him to kick rocks and leave me alone because we're celebrating my brother's wedding and I'm the maid of honor. But tonight, with the way he's looking at me and the heat his body is throwing, I quickly say, "Yes."

Plus, there's the whiskey.

Dreamboat smiles.

I pull away, getting a better look at his face. It's sheer and utter perfection. His honey-brown eyes are only the beginning of what I'd call insanely hot with a dash of let-me-ride-that-face sexy. His square jawline is dotted with just the right amount of stubble to tickle my inner thighs, and his full lips are made for kissing.

This was the first wedding where I didn't expect to

hook up with anyone. Every person in the wedding party was related to me in some way, which left the guests. With hundreds of relatives and people from the neighborhood, I didn't see any orgasms on the horizon when the evening began. But now there's Dreamboat, filling the void of what very well could've ended up being a lonely and miserably drunk night in my hotel room.

Dreamboat licks his lips. I can't stop myself from watching the slow, torturous path of his tongue across his mouth. I should ask his name, but in this moment, I don't really care. He could be named Clyde, and I'd still roll around in the sack with him for a night.

That's the thing about one-night stands...details don't matter—actions do. And based on the way he's holding me and his eyes are blazing, I'm fairly certain he'd be nothing short of spec-fucking-tacular in the sack.

No one notices as we slip into the hallway. Dreamboat's hand is on my back, guiding me through the lobby. I steal a glance his way, risking falling on my face again.

He's staring straight ahead with his chin up, oozing confidence and a whole lotta swagger.

The tailored suit hugs his body in all the right places and is loaded with muscles.

"Wait, I can't just leave like this." I turn to him when we're within feet of the hotel bar, rethinking my stupid decision after coming to my senses. "It's my brother's wedding, and I'm the maid of honor. I can't just ditch everyone."

Dreamboat doesn't even flinch. "You go back. I'll wait," he tells me.

My stomach flutters with the way he's looking at me and the promise of the pleasure he'll no doubt deliver. "Don't do that. It could be hours. If we're meant to be, we'll see each other again," I tell him, drinking in his rugged handsomeness as I step backward and somehow don't end up on my ass.

I'm clearly intoxicated because who says that kind of ridiculous crap.

The answer would be me when I'm plastered.

I leave him standing in the lobby and march away on shaky legs, fanning myself as I head straight back to the ballroom without so much as a backward glance.

The wedding's still in full swing when I step through the double doors. Aunt Fran is dancing on top of the table near the doorway, and a small crowd has assembled to watch her impressive moves. Bear's laughing and trying to get her to come down before the wobbly table collapses, but she bats him away and twists her hips wildly, not giving two shits.

"Happens every damn time," Morgan says as he comes to stand next to me. "She can't hold her liquor."

We stare at his mother, but I can't stop smiling. "I like your mom. Cut her some slack. Someday we'll be old too, and I hope we have enough energy to do that." I motion toward her as she squats down, shaking her ass like she's in a rap video and totally dropping it like it's hot.

"So fucking embarrassing." Morgan covers his eyes with his hand and groans before wandering away.

"Will the bride and groom please come to the dance floor? You know what time it is," the DJ announces, turning the attention away from Fran.

I hate this part of the wedding. There's something so archaic about the throwing of the garter and the bouquet. All the single people at the wedding line up like cattle, exposing our lack of love and our desperation to get hitched someday, with everything hinging on catching an object we'll throw in the trash the next day.

The guests cheer as Lucio and Delilah make their way to the dance floor, holding each other's hand as they walk. They're so happy and so in love, I'm almost a little jealous. I always thought I'd be married by now. I never for one moment figured Lucio would get hitched before me. The man swore off relationships from the day he discovered pussy, but here we are... at his wedding.

Michelle spots me from across the room and makes a beeline in my direction. The ruffled mess Delilah calls a dress looks so much better on Michelle. Her tiny waist and big tits are no match for the layers. And her blond hair, pulled back in a tight bun, shows off her long neck line, her soft facial features just adding to the perfection. "Where the hell did you go?" she asks and points toward the hallway.

"I stepped out for a minute."

The fewer details I give her, the better. I already feel like shit for leaving my brother's wedding, even if it was only for a few minutes.

Michelle's head jerks back like I slapped her. "Stepped out?"

I nod and make a face. I thought my words were pretty self-explanatory. I wasn't about to say I was trying to get my brains banged right out of my head by an absolute stranger before I finally came to my senses.

She puts her hands on her hips, and I know she's about to grill me. "With who? Where?"

"I went to the lobby for some fresh air." I'm lying, but the words slide off my tongue so easily, I even believe my own bullshit for a hot second.

She cocks her head to the side and narrows her eyes. "Who's the guy?" she asks without missing a beat, knowing me better than I know myself sometimes.

That's how it is between us. We've been best friends since we still had training wheels on our Huffys. We were, and always have been, inseparable. In a family filled with men, she's the closest thing I have to a sister and the person who knows all my secrets.

"There's no guy."

I'm sticking to my story. There's no way I'm coming clean.

She ticks her chin in my direction, eyeing something behind me. "Then, who's he?" She crosses her arms and tilts her head, letting me know I'm very much caught.

Shit.

I don't want to turn around. That would be totally obvious. By the way Michelle's looking at whoever is behind me, they know we're talking about them already. No need to fan the flames of embarrassment.

"What do they look like?"

"Tall, dark, handsome, and wearing a suit."

I roll my eyes. "Jesus, Michelle. You just described every man in this room. Be a little more specific."

"Just look," she tells me.

Like it's that easy.

"What color eyes does he have?"

"Seriously?" She shakes her head, and I know she's judging me. "Did you leave with more than one guy or something?"

"No, no. It's not like that."

"Well, prepare yourself. He's walking toward us and..."

"Daphne." The shivers from earlier skate across my skin, and I know Dreamboat's behind me.

I turn my head and smile. "Hey," I say casually because I don't want him to know what he does to me or for Michelle to think something more happened than the tragic truth of my sad, lonely vagina missing out on what I'd assume would be numerous orgasms.

27

"Can we talk?" he asks, without even looking at Michelle.

"Give me a minute," I tell Michelle and place my hand on her arm, hoping she doesn't make a scene.

She stares at me for a second before glancing at Dreamboat over my shoulder. "He looks familiar."

"He's one of Lucio's buddies," I tell her.

In all honesty, I have no clue who he is, and a few minutes ago, I didn't really care.

"Be careful." She places her hand over mine. "With your father back, people are going to come out of the woodwork."

"But it's a wedding."

"There's no safe time or place when Santino's around," she reminds me.

That's the cold, hard reality of my father's line of work. There's always a willing someone out there, thinking about putting a bullet in our heads as payback for some fucked-up thing our father did.

"I won't leave with him. I promise."

She stares at Dreamboat for a moment before walking toward the dance floor where Lucio currently has his head up Delilah's dress, making a spectacle of retrieving the garter and taking his sweet-ass time too.

I turn to face the man I very well could've been naked with if it weren't for my regaining my sanity. "Who are you?"

Dreamboat doesn't seem frazzled by my question. He has one hand in his pants pocket and the other at his side, standing tall and just as confident as ever. "I'm Leo," he answers, like his name should clue me the fuck in on something.

I don't touch him, but I want to. I like being near him. I like the way my body reacts when he touches me, and I hate myself for it. "One of Lucio's friends?"

Leo shakes his head.

"Delilah's?"

He shakes his head again.

"Well," I say, wasting time because I'm confused, and the whiskey doesn't make anything easier.

If he's not friends with Lucio or Delilah, then why the hell is he here? Then it hits me. Maybe he's a relative.

Jesus, please don't make him family.

"Cousin?" I grimace, hoping like hell he'll shake his head again.

Leo shakes his head again, ending the possibility that I almost banged my own blood.

Thank fuck.

"I know your father," he says casually, like it's not a big freaking deal.

This can't be happening.

I want to slap myself in the face...repeatedly. Out of all the men at the wedding, I had to almost hook up with someone who associates with my father. A mobster and an ex-con.

Yippee.

I should seriously get the gold star for this one.

By the looks of Leo, he totally fits the mold of the smooth, handsome, and irresistible bad-boy gangster Hollywood has always portrayed.

"My father invited you?"

I didn't even know my father was out of prison until he showed his face tonight. But clearly, other people knew, including Leo.

"Not exactly," Leo replies, being cagey.

I cross my arms over my chest, unable to stop myself from staring at this hot-as-fuck guy. And when I say hot-as-fuck, I mean off-the-charts, panty-melting, ride-him-until-I-die kind of sexiness.

"You're friends with my father, and you tried to sleep with me. That's fucked up."

Leo smirks. "I never said I was his friend."

At this point, I'm confused and too drunk to form any type of rational thoughts. I don't have time to ask any more questions because Johnny, my father's friend and business associate, is heading straight for us.

He doesn't look happy, but then again, Johnny's rarely sporting a smile.

"Look out," I say, because if Leo isn't my father's friend, Johnny isn't coming to say hello.

Leo turns around, and his cocky smirk vanishes as soon as he lays eyes on Johnny. "I better go."

But before he can move, Johnny is so close to Leo, they're practically standing nose-to-nose. "I'm going to be nice about this because we're at a wedding," Johnny says, staring Leo straight in the eye and almost foaming at the mouth.

Oh shit. This isn't good.

Leo doesn't seem fazed by the way Johnny's gritting his teeth like a dog ready to attack. "I was just leaving," Leo tells him.

"You have some balls showing up here, kid." Johnny pushes his fingers through his gray hair, smoothing back the sides.

Leo squares his shoulders, not backing down. "I wanted to see with my own eyes." He's not afraid of Johnny. That much is clear.

"Don't come near Tino's family." Johnny's eyes slice to me, and I know he doesn't like me talking to Leo.

I'm eventually going to get an earful, but it has always been hard to keep up with who's who in the Chicago mob world.

"Especially his daughter. She's off-limits."

His words don't sit well with me. My father's business has nothing to do with me or my life. He stopped calling the shots somewhere around the time he went to the joint for my entire middle school years. But that doesn't stop Johnny from trying to run my life.

"Johnny, I'm grown. I can make that choice," I tell him with one hand on my hip, throwing him tons of shade.

Johnny's eyes darken immediately. I can see he doesn't agree. "Do you have a death wish, Daphne?"

"Who's going to off me?" My eyes slice to Leo the dreamboat. "Leo?" I laugh nervously.

Leo has been a complete gentleman. Well, if you don't count trying to get me up to his room to fuck my brains out not that long ago.

"You know who Mario Conti is, right?"

It's hard not to know Mario. He and my father were friends back in the day until Mario decided to split from the family and form his own. Since that day, my father and Mario have been mortal enemies.

"Uh, yeah, Johnny. I know the name well."

Johnny pitches his head toward Leo. "This is his kid."

I gawk at Leo, wondering if he was, in fact, going to off me as soon as we were alone. The thought doesn't seem as wild and stupid as it did a few seconds ago. Was there a hit on me? Jesus, the thought sends chills down my spine.

"Were you going to..." My voice drifts off. I can't seem to bring myself to say the words. They're horrifying.

Leo shakes his head. "I only had one thing on my mind."

"Get the fuck out," Johnny says and points toward the door. "You have thirty seconds to get your feet moving, or I'll toss you out on your ass. Wedding or no wedding, I will make an example of you."

"Johnny." I draw his attention back to me as I touch his arm. I want to talk to Leo alone without my father's henchman nearby. "Give us a minute, and then he'll leave. Don't make a scene at my brother's wedding. Please."

Johnny stares at me but doesn't move or speak for a moment. I think he's going to fight me on this, but he doesn't. "Thirty seconds," he says before he steps backward, keeping his eyes on Leo until he's a few feet away.

"I can't believe you."

Anger, rage, and hurt well up inside me.

How could I have been so stupid?

"Daphne, listen." Leo's dark eyes bore into me, and that sexy, sinful look from earlier seems more sinister with the knowledge of who he is. "I wasn't going to hurt you."

"Mm-hmm." I'm not convinced.

Leo reaches between us and takes my hand in his. The warmth of his palm sends tiny bolts of lightning throughout my system, and I instantly wish everything could be different. The way he looks at me is unlike how any man has ever looked at me before. Maybe it's not sexual like I'd imagined, but filled with rage and hatred instead.

He sweeps his thumb across the top of my hand in slow, steady strokes. "I like you. I like you a lot, and that's dangerous for both of us."

Well, that's the understatement of the year.

"Right now, you're the only one in danger." I pull my hand away even though I like the way he touches me. Then there's his face. Damn, Leo's all kinds of sexy, and it kills me to say my next words. "Just go, Leo. Go before you ruin my brother's wedding."

"See me again," he begs.

Everything in me wants to say yes, but then I see Johnny giving me the stink eye, looking like he's about to go all Tony Montana on Leo. "It's better if you keep your distance. I don't date mobsters anyway."

"I'm a businessman."

"Sure, you are. And I'm Mother Teresa."

"We're not done. I'll find you," he promises.

I don't know if I should be excited about that statement or scared to death.

CHAPTER THREE

DAPHNE

My head throbs as I pull the sheet over my face, trying to block out the sunlight streaming through the annoying little slit in the curtains. My tongue sticks to the roof of my mouth as I try to swallow, getting the first taste, which I'm not sure any amount of brushing will ever wipe away.

Last night, I had way too much to drink. I totally blame Morgan for continuing to ply me with alcohol long after Leo left. Aunt Fran was partially to blame because she got the ball rolling with the bottles of whiskey, sabotaging my plans to stay sober.

"You're awake," a deep, gravelly voice says beside me.

I freeze as my eyes widen.

Who the fuck is next to me?

I knew I was trashed, but I didn't think I'd had so many shots I wouldn't remember inviting someone back to my hotel room, but clearly, I did.

Lying here, thinking about last night, I remember being at the reception, laughing with my cousins. But for the life of me, I don't remember walking through the lobby, the ride up in the elevator, or the last few steps to my room.

Shit.

This could be bad.

Like, really bad.

I squeeze my eyes shut and say a silent prayer, hoping like hell I didn't sleep with one of my brother's friends. Either way...this has to be my dumbest moment of my entire life.

Well, at least the second dumbest because that time under the football stadium bleachers with Tommy Pasquale probably takes the cake. But I've blocked that memory out for so long, I refuse to breathe a whisper of it to another human being for the rest of my life.

Maybe the guy and I passed out, and neither of us will remember a thing about last night. That would be the best scenario at this point. I can at least hope that will be the case. Maybe he was so drunk he couldn't even get it up, or I'll find him completely dressed and on top of the sheets because he was a complete gentleman.

A hand slides across my bare thigh and puts all doubt and hope I have to rest. "Please, God," I whisper.

Rarely has the Almighty come to my aid, but there's never been a time I needed him more than right now.

The bed dips as the stranger rolls closer. When his bare skin touches mine, I know my prayers have most certainly not been answered. By the way his morning wood is digging into my thigh, I can probably assume we fucked too.

"Morning, *bella*," he says.

Oh shit. For real? I close my eyes again, and flashes of leaving the hotel come flooding back like giant slaps in the face in that perfect spot that makes you feel like your skull's going to explode.

My entire body goes rigid. Leo's naked. I'm naked. His cock is touching me, and I can't remember a damn thing.

Just great.

"Did we...?" I suddenly feel ill.

I don't give him time to answer. I don't even care I'm naked as I roll off the bed and run toward the bathroom, knowing I'm about to hurl every single thing that could possibly be left in my stomach into the toilet.

Leaning over the porcelain goddess, I gag, waiting to vomit, but nothing comes. My chest heaves, and tears sting my eyes with the realization I've fucked up by sleeping with him.

Not just a little, but so damn big.

After growing up surrounded by men who easily could've walked straight out of *The Sopranos*, I told myself I'd never get involved with anyone in the family *business*.

My father ruined the sexiness Hollywood had portrayed. I knew the lifestyle wasn't as glamorous as many people believed. Besides that, mobsters were dangerous as fuck. But out of all the guys in Chicago, why the hell did I have to sleep with one who's the son of my father's enemy?

The tears fall fast and hard as the stupidity of the entire situation hits me.

"You okay in there?" Leo asks from the other side of the door.

I can't help myself. I start to laugh as the tears plop onto the seat of the toilet, popping like my shame.

The doorknob jiggles. "I'm coming in."

"No!" I yell and bite down on my lip, trying to stop the giggles that have suddenly taken over. "I'm fine. Go away."

"No, *bella*. Not until I know you're okay."

"I'm fine. Just fucking great." I start to laugh louder than before and slip, falling backward and hitting my back against the bathtub. I howl like an injured wild animal as the edge digs into my skin.

Leo doesn't bother asking if I'm okay again before

he barges through the bathroom door in all his naked glory.

Well, damn.

My laughter dies. I gawk at his body. My face is covered with tears, both from pain and embarrassment, and I'm as naked as the day I was born.

I'm a mess and in pain, but damn it...the man is fine.

Thick, muscular thighs. Abs that resemble an old-fashioned washboard, complete with the most perfect happy trail, which leads to a long and perfectly thick cock. His pecs are even off-the-charts hot. The man is built. Then there's his face. His dark eyes, full lips, stubble, and somehow, he pulls off bed head.

Goddammit, why does he have to be nothing short of perfection?

"Jesus." Leo scoops me into his arms, not waiting for me to ask for help.

I'm about to slap his hands away, but my back aches and then there's the fact that I'm so hungover, I'm not sure I could make it back to the bed while staying upright.

"Are you hurt?"

I don't answer.

His hot skin against mine is doing crazy shit to my insides and totally scrambling my brain. I've never been that girl. The one rendered speechless by a guy. Somehow, I've turned into her, and Leo Conti's to blame.

He places my bottom on the bed and then starts to inspect my body for any damage. Leo's hand skates across my skin while I'm face-to-face with his cock. I don't mean it's nearby. I mean, if I stick my tongue out, I'll get a taste.

I can't make myself look away either.

He may be my father's enemy, but that doesn't mean I can't appreciate the man and his off-the-charts hotness along with the sheer perfection of his dick. This is by far the biggest clusterfuck of my life.

"I'm fine, Leo," I lie and cover my face with my hands, totally embarrassed and wishing I could get a do-over. "You should go," I tell him and try to keep my eyes on his face instead of his beautiful cock.

If anyone in my family catches Leo in my room, it'll be game over for both of us.

He backs up, his cock waving around like it's taunting me, and places his hands on his hips. "This is my place. Where do you want me to go?"

Fuck my life.

"Why me?" I groan and drag my fingers down my face.

Leo kneels in front of me and pushes my hands away. "You don't remember, do you?"

"I remember," I say quickly, completely defensive.

I don't want to be *that* girl.

You know...the type I clearly am.

The corner of his mouth turns upward. "Tell me what position we did it in?"

I laugh and wince all at once because the tiny monster inside my head is jackhammering away like a boss, probably etching the word "Whiskey" onto my skull as a reminder. "Come on. That's so easy," I scoff.

He raises an eyebrow. "Then tell me."

I mentally flip through every possibility as quick as I can. Since I was drunk off my ass, there's a high likelihood I wasn't on top because...hello, I could barely walk.

Leo doesn't look like the missionary type of guy either, so that's right out the window immediately.

Two down and only a few hundred to go.

"Doggy," I blurt out. I'm almost positive this guy is an ass man. If ass men had a look, they'd be Leo.

The smirk on his face turns into a full-on smile as he shakes his head.

"Against the wall," I say, trying again. When Leo shakes his head again, I know there's no way I can go on pretending that I can remember any goddamn second of last night. "Fine. I don't remember." I feel all kinds of whorish, like I need to run to the nearest church and beg for forgiveness in the confessional.

"You're cute." He slides his massive hand against my cheek and cups my face. "I didn't think you were that drunk, or else..."

I glance away, trying to avoid his dark, penetrating gaze. "Now, he has morals," I say before he can finish the statement.

"Hey," he says, drawing my eyes back to his. "I

always have morals, especially when it comes to women."

Suddenly, I realize how very naked I am. I was so taken by his bare skin, I completely forgot I wasn't wearing a stitch of clothing and had done nothing to shield myself.

"Fuck." I push his hand away and scramble to my feet, taking the top sheet off the bed with me. Wrapping the material around my body, I glance around the room, trying to find the monstrosity I wore last night. "Where's my dress?"

He pitches his head toward the door. "In the living room."

Living room?

"You have a suite?"

He shakes his head, and that cocky, drop-dead-sexy smirk is back. "We're at my place."

"I've got to go." I rush toward the door, not giving two fucks about anything except getting the hell out of here.

Leo wraps his hand around my arm and hauls me backward. "Don't you want a few memories to take with you?" There's a smug grin on his face.

I glance down to where his hand is against my skin and grind my teeth. "You want to keep your cock?" I raise an eyebrow as I gaze up into his eyes.

"You're feisty. I like it," he teases before he releases his grip on my arm. "Tiger through and through." I know he's loving every moment of my misery.

I don't even have time to ask what the fuck that means. I'm all kinds of sideways. "Pretend I don't exist." I run out of his bedroom, scrambling to find my dress to get the fuck out of his place.

Leo leans against the wall in the living room as I scoop my dress off the floor.

I drop the sheet, giving him a full view because he's seen it all anyway. "Get your last look." I yank the dress over my head.

Leo's standing there, arms crossed, looking all kinds of sexy, with his cock waving in appreciation.

"It's the last time you'll see me," I tell him.

"*Bella*." He closes the space between us in three quick strides before taking my chin between two of his fingers. "You made promises last night."

I gawk at him, blinking uncontrollably and totally lost. "What?" I ask him, not exactly knowing what the fuck he even means by that statement. "I was drunk. You can't hold me accountable for anything I said or did."

He slides his finger against my jaw as his thumb comes to a rest behind my ear. "It means we aren't done. Not by a long shot," he tells me, like he's making all the sense in the world, and somehow, I'm just supposed to agree.

My eyes are locked on his. I can't bring myself to look away, no matter how hard I try. "We can't do this again, Leo."

"We won't. Next time, you'll be sober and begging for my touch."

Butterflies start to buzz around my stomach at his words. Or maybe it's the liquor still sloshing around, waiting for its perfect moment to remind me of all the ways I fucked up. I swallow down every bit of lust this man fuels in me and lift my chin, ever defiant.

He leans forward like he's about to kiss me. I hold my breath, wanting him to both do it and not at all at the same time.

I pull away, moving quickly toward the door, and I glance over my shoulder. "Forget I exist."

"We're not done, *bella*," he tells me as the door closes.

CHAPTER FOUR

DAPHNE

MICHELLE CALLS as I'm trying to pull myself together and somehow make myself presentable for the family luncheon at the bar.

"Whore, where did you disappear to last night?" she asks, because Michelle's nosy as fuck.

"I didn't feel well, so I went to bed early."

"I knocked on your hotel room this morning, but you didn't answer."

She's fishing, but I'm not biting.

"I passed out and didn't hear you."

"Let me walk down there now."

"No!" My voice comes out much louder than I intend. I know I have to cover my tracks and quick. "I already left. I wanted to shower at home before heading to the bar."

There's a pause, and I know she's about to call bullshit. "Hmm," Michelle grunts. "I could've sworn I saw you leave with that guy from last night."

I drop my head forward, wishing she would've just come out and said something to begin with. "You're an asshole."

She laughs on the other end of the phone. "I wanted to see what cockamamie story you'd come up with."

"I was so freaking drunk. Why did you let me leave with him?"

"I tried to stop you. I called your name, but you seemed oblivious to everything and everyone except for him."

"What a fucking disaster."

"Well, we've all been there. It's done now. Move on."

"Michelle, that's the thing." I stare into the mirror, giving myself the look my mother used to give me when she was disappointed in my behavior. "You know who he is, right?"

"The hot guy?" She pauses for a second. "Nope."

"Leo Conti."

She gasps. "Shut the fuck up."

"Yep."

"Stop fucking lying to me."

"It's true. God, I wish I were lying," I groan.

"You seriously fucked Mario Conti's kid?"

"Yeah," I whisper and toss my eyeliner pencil back in the drawer. "But that kid is all man." There's no way I can focus enough to avoid looking like someone out of those *How Not to Apply Makeup* videos on the internet.

"You know that's messed up, right?"

"I don't get involved in my father's world. I drank too much. That's my only defense."

"Daphne." I can picture her shaking her head at my sheer stupidity. "Stay away from that man. His father and your father..."

"I know. I know. I don't have plans to ever see him again."

"Was he good, at least?"

"I don't know. I don't remember." I wince as I say the words.

"That's a shame." Michelle laughs. "There's going to be blowback eventually, and it would be nice at least to have a fond memory or two to look back on."

"Shut up. He said he's a businessman. I don't really know anything about him except I made an epic mistake."

"Did he at least have a bangin' body underneath that suit?"

"The best I've ever seen," I say honestly.

"Better than Tommy Pasquale?"

He follows me everywhere.

"Girl, better than any male on the planet."

"Big dick?"

"Perfect. Long and thick."

"Fuck. All the good ones are either taken, unavailable, or off-limits. I swear, it's tough out here."

"From your lips to God's ears." I pull on my sandals, wishing my mother would've canceled Sunday dinner, but that's not her style. "I got to run. I'll see you at work tonight, yeah?"

"I'm going to do some digging before I come in."

"No. Absolutely not. Do not ask around about him, Michelle. I don't want our names linked even in casual conversation."

But I know, no matter what I say, Michelle's going to stick her nose right where it doesn't belong. That's what we do for each other, and it's why she's my best friend. She always has my back. Always. Doesn't matter if I'm in the wrong, she's willing to go down with the ship.

"I'll be discreet," she promises before hanging up.

I'm not sure she even understands what that word means.

An hour later, I'm at the bar, and my father is standing in the middle of the room, clinking his fork against his wineglass to get everyone's attention.

This isn't a normal Sunday dinner. My mother decided to invite the out of town guests to the bar for one last hurrah to close out the wedding weekend.

Thankfully, she didn't cook and was smart enough to have the event catered from Dino's down the street.

"First, I want to thank everyone for coming to celebrate with us. We're overjoyed to have Delilah as part of our family." My father pauses and glances down at my mother, who's beaming from ear to ear. "Second, as the years pass by, Betty and I understand how important family is, and we wanted you to be the first to know we have officially decided to tie the knot."

"You've got to be kidding me," I mutter under my breath, which earns me a kick under the table from Angelo.

"Seriously, Angelo." I stare at him, arms crossed, totally annoyed. "Why now? You can't be happy about this."

My parents have been together over thirty years, but they have never once seriously talked about getting married until this moment. It makes no sense. The time to do it was decades ago when they decided to start a family, not after we're all already grown.

"It makes total sense. They're getting older, Daph."

Angelo's words don't sit well with me. I know the years are ticking by, but I still can't think of my parents as old. Even though they both drive me crazy at times, I can't imagine a world without them in it.

"I need some air."

I quietly excuse myself from the table and slip into the back alleyway without anyone noticing. I'm leaning against the wall, scrolling through my social media and catching up on all the funny cat videos I've missed, when my father steps outside too.

We stare at each other for a minute and don't speak.

The last words I uttered to my father before they took him away in handcuffs were not the most heart-warming.

In my defense, I was angry.

What girl wouldn't be when her father's about to be locked up for years because of a choice he made, fully knowing the consequences?

My father runs his fingers through his salt-and-pepper hair and stares at the ground as he kicks some gravel. "Hey, baby girl. How are you doing?"

"I'm fine." I tuck my phone into my back pocket and try to be cordial. "Why aren't you inside with your guests?"

He finally brings his eyes to mine. "I wanted to check on you." He ticks his head toward the door. "I saw you run out of there."

"I just needed some air."

"Want me to go?"

"No," I say quickly.

"Still mad after all these years?" he asks.

"I don't know what I am, Papa," I answer honestly.

Part of me is happy that he's okay and back under the same roof as my mother. But then there's the other part that knows he's just going to be up to his old tricks soon enough, possibly landing back in prison. Each time, he seems to stay out a little longer than before, which has never been easy for anyone, especially my mother.

"You guys have done really well with the bar," he tells me, changing the subject.

"We've worked a lot of hours."

He comes to stand in front of me. It's my first real chance to get a good look at my father with the sun shining overhead.

My brothers get their good looks from my father. The rich olive skin, the piercing eyes, and strong Gallo features. My father's DNA is definitely more dominant than my mother's. I could've very easily had red hair and ivory skin instead of looking every bit the Italian princess.

"Don't forget to enjoy life a little. It passes in the blink of an eye. One day you're young, thinking you can rule the world, and the next thing you know... Bam!" He smacks his hands together, making me jump. "You're praying you make it just one more day."

This is a side of my father I haven't seen before. He's always taken life by the balls without a single care about the consequences. He's never really discussed getting older, but maybe five years with nothing but time to think will do that to a person.

"What about you, Papa? Do you have another five years in you to spend behind bars?"

My father reaches out and places his hands on my shoulders, much like he did when I was a little girl.

"Time is too precious, Daphne. I don't want to spend another moment away from my family."

"But?" I can feel there's more to what he's saying. There usually is when it comes to my father. He talks around things, always avoiding what he really wants to say.

"There's no buts."

There's always a but with Santino Gallo.

"You're giving up the life? Going straight?"

The small dimple on his right cheek deepens. "Something like that, kid."

"You either are, or you aren't." I'm point-blank, unwilling to dance around my father's statement.

"I learned a thing or two in the joint."

That's exactly what I was afraid he'd say. Spending five years surrounded by nothing but criminals has to allow someone an opportunity to hone their skills a little bit more. I'm sure he picked up some tricks of the trade, but he needs to remember, every guy in there wasn't smart enough to avoid being arrested.

"I promised your mom I wouldn't go back." When he speaks, he doesn't look me in the eye. "I'm going to stay clean. Be on the up-and-up."

"I really hope so." I mean those words.

There's nothing I want more than to have my father around. If for no other reason than to be there for my mother.

I worry about her being alone.

The last five years have been hard on her. She

found hobbies to take up her time, but there's only so many things a person can make before they hit their breaking point.

I wait for him to release me, but he doesn't. He stares at me, pulling me into a tight embrace. "I missed my baby girl," he whispers in my ear.

I feel like a little girl again. I'm hopeful for a minute. Thinking maybe my father has finally grown up, but then I remember he's rarely truthful and getting out of the life is hard, especially for an old-timer like him.

"I missed you too," I tell him because I did miss having him around. Even though he adds a special brand of insanity, the bar and Sunday dinners haven't been the same without him.

"Come celebrate with us," he says, still holding me tightly.

"When's the big day?" I ask out of morbid curiosity.

"We're not rushing into anything."

Of course they aren't because that would be totally absurd. Only my father would think getting married sooner rather than later would be rushing into something. I swear they've had the longest courtship on the planet.

"It's only been thirty years, Papa." I shake my head as I start to laugh.

"What's on your neck?" He leans forward and brushes my hair off my shoulder.

"I don't know. What is it?" I turn my head, giving him a better look.

"It looks like a hickey." He moves closer, inspecting my skin like he used to after I had a date. "It *is* a hickey."

Son of a...

My eyes widen. I know exactly who left me with a sucker bite like we were in high school. "Jesus," I mutter and instantly want to track Leo down and punch him square in his junk.

"I didn't know you were seeing someone."

I look at the ground, avoiding my father's eyes and any chance I'll tell him the truth. "I'm not." I cover the mark with my palm and take a step backward. "Someone was just being an asshole."

"What's his name?" he asks, trying to be fatherly for the first time in over five years.

"We better get inside. I'm sure everyone's looking for us," I say, trying to avoid the conversation entirely.

All I need is for my father to hear the name Leo Conti.

His head would probably explode.

CHAPTER FIVE

DAPHNE

I'M STARTLED awake by rustling on the fire escape outside my bedroom window. Last night, I slept with my window open and the curtains pulled closed, foolishly thinking I'd be safe. I should've known better. But the night's cool air was too hard to resist in my second-floor loft.

Reaching under the pillow, I wrap my fingers around the cold steel handle of a gun. I always keep it there just in case.

I roll onto the floor, thinking I look like someone in an action movie, but I realize I'm missing the sexy swagger. My knees dig into the hardwood, and I grit my teeth, trying to stop myself from crying. As I crawl toward the window, I'm barely breathing, trying not to make a sound.

I crouch down, aiming the gun toward the curtains and resting my finger on the trigger just in case the visitor decides to come inside. Maybe I'm totally over-reacting, but I'm not willing to take any chances, especially with my father now walking the streets.

A black leather shoe peeks through the curtains, and I stiffen immediately. "Hold it right there. I have a gun," I yell, but my voice quivers. I'm holding the gun out in front of me, ready to shoot whoever this dumbass is if he moves another inch.

The person freezes. "Don't shoot," he says quickly, and the sound of his voice sends goose bumps scattering across my skin.

I lift my finger off the trigger and let out a heavy sigh. I could've killed him. Not figuratively, but actually killed Leo Conti because he had to crawl through my window like a stalker and a freaking idiot. "What the hell are you doing here?"

"Can I move now?" Leo asks, still frozen with only a foot inside my place and the rest of his body hidden behind the curtains.

"Yes. I won't shoot you... Well, not yet, at least."

The curtains part, and Leo's head comes through the window, followed by his other half. He's dressed in a pristine suit, looking every bit as fuckable as he did on Saturday night.

"Why are you here?" I ask, still pointing the gun at him. Both turned on by his presence and wanting to shoot him too for scaring the shit out of me.

His eyes slowly rake over my body, drinking in every inch of my bare flesh. "That answers that."

"Answers what?"

He rubs the pad of his thumb down the corner of his mouth, looking all hot and shit. "If you sleep naked all the time." He smirks.

I glance down, my heart still pounding, and I'm so filled with adrenaline, I totally forgot I was buck-ass naked.

I place my free hand on my hip and look him up and down, much the same way he's looking at me. "Are you trying to make me shoot you?" I cock an eyebrow.

He takes a step toward me. "God, you're sexy as fuck."

I back up. "Don't change the subject." I want him way too much, and I need to do everything in my power to avoid his touch. "What the hell are you doing here?"

"I wanted to talk." He doesn't stop moving toward me.

The backs of my knees hit the mattress, and I have nowhere else to go. "How about knocking like a normal person?"

He covers the gun with his hand, pulling the cool metal from my grip. "It's too dangerous."

"Crawling through my window isn't exactly safe." I motion to my gun which is now safely in his hand and ignore the fact that our bodies are almost touching. "I could've killed you."

Honest to God, I was two seconds from pulling the trigger. The mess his death could've created would've been astronomical. How would I have explained why Leo Conti was crawling through my window?

"That'd be pretty hard since the safety's on."

I grunt and purse my lips. "I still could've shot you. It's not that difficult to take the safety off."

His eyes twinkle. "I'll take my chances with you over them." He pitches his head toward the window.

"Them?"

Leo leans forward, and I hold my breath, thinking he's going to kiss me. Even though I know it's a horrible idea, my belly flips and my body tingles, wanting his lips on mine way too much.

Instead, he places the gun on the bed behind me. "There are too many eyes on both of us." As he rights himself, the back of his hand brushes against my thigh, whisper-soft.

I shudder and am suddenly breathless, both from the tidbit of information he just dropped in my lap and his touch. "There's no one watching me," I argue.

He tilts his head and says nothing more, but the look he gives me says everything I need to know.

"Seriously?" My mouth falls open. "I've never seen anyone."

"There's always people watching us, Daphne. Our fathers are too important for us to go unguarded or unnoticed."

I always knew my father had protection, but I never really thought about someone watching over me or my brothers.

"Then I better put some clothes on." I start to move, but Leo reaches out and grabs my hand.

"Let's not panic," he tells me as his fingertips scorch my flesh.

He's the enemy.

I repeat that statement over and over again as Leo stares at me with those dreamy, sinful eyes.

I glance down, staring at the spot where our skin touches, and I know I need to take drastic measures. "Move it or lose it."

"What are you going to do, little girl?" he taunts as he swipes his thumb across the underside of my wrist.

I don't know what kind of women he's used to being around, but the one thing I'm not is weak. Growing up with three brothers and a father who didn't live on the up-and-up made it almost impossible for me to be a damsel in distress or anyone's victim. I could punch like a guy and take down a man twice my size without breaking a sweat. It didn't matter that I was naked; I could still put his ass on the floor.

"I'd hate to wrinkle your fancy suit," I tell him,

giving him a once-over before staring him straight in the eyes. The corner of Leo's mouth twitches before he finally releases me. "I'll ask again, why are you here, Leo?"

"I wanted to see you again."

"Well, you saw me. All of me...again." I point toward the door. "So, you can go now."

Leo's eyes narrow as he closes any remaining space between us. I hold my breath as he reaches out and brushes a few strands of hair behind my back with his fingers. Even though my breasts are inches from his face, his eyes are locked on mine and nowhere else.

"We're not done," he tells me again.

I can't help but stare back at him.

"There's no we, Leo. There never will be. There never can be. Whatever happened, happened. We'll leave it at that. Two drunk people fucked. End of story. No big deal."

Leo's eyes darken, and he grips my wrist again, tethering himself to me. I know I should pull away, but there's something about the way he's looking at me that makes moving impossible. "First of all, I wasn't drunk."

"So, you took advantage of me? A drunk chick. Nice." I know it's a complete lie. He didn't take advantage of me. I can guarantee I was more than willing. But I'm sticking to that as the reason why I slept with the son of my father's mortal enemy.

"*Bella*." He sweeps his hand under my hair and rests his palm against my neck. "Nothing happened."

I'm not even listening to him. I'm too upset, mostly at myself, to even hear what he's saying. "Hell, only a sleazebag would fuck a drunk girl."

His tongue pokes out, dragging slowly across his bottom lip. I watch the smooth movement with my lips parted, making it impossible for me to deny the attraction much longer.

His fingers dig into the back of my neck, just below my hair, sending shock waves down my spine. "Daphne, I'm going to repeat this, and you're going to be quiet and listen."

I blink, taken aback by his bossiness and a little turned on.

"We went back to my place to talk. We made out a little bit, but you were so tired, you undressed in my living room and walked—well, mostly staggered—to my bed and collapsed. Nothing happened. I didn't take advantage of you."

"Oh." I stare into his eyes and then realize he's been lying to me. "Wait. What?"

"I'm not a sleazebag."

"Okay." I nod. I don't know what else to do or say. I feel like an asshole, but come on, anyone in my shoes would've thought the same damn thing.

"I feel like shit that you left thinking we had sex. I needed to talk to you, and I want to take you on a real date."

With the way he's holding me and how he's looking at me, thinking isn't easy. "You what?"

Leo's hot.

Like *GQ* hot with a dash of *Godfather*. Dark hair, dark eyes, lush mouth, and built for riding. He's totally my dream man, minus the fact that we could never be together and his cocky attitude leaves something to be desired...most of the time.

"I want one date, and then I'll leave you alone."

"That's all?"

Going on a date with Leo Conti wouldn't be the worst thing in the world. I'd done crazier shit for men who were not at the same freakishly hot level as Leo. I take that back. They were all hot, but some weren't too bright. Those were the ones I had put up with long enough to go one round, or sometimes two, in the sack before pushing them away, which was pretty easy and comical.

"If you never want to see me again after that, I promise to go away forever."

"One date," I whisper as my belly flutters. "But how? If we're being watched, that would be damn near impossible."

"You let me worry about that, sweetheart."

I have a few triggers, and men calling me by pet names when they don't even know me is one. Most women would think it's charming, but not me.

"Let's get one thing straight. I'm not your sweetheart, your baby, your doll, or your anything. Got it?"

Leo smirks. "I got it, *bella*."

I'm about to reply and tell him off, but before I can,

Leo leans forward. My breath hitches as his lips come near mine. I'm staring into his eyes, unable to breathe, waiting for the moment his soft lips touch mine. Wanting it more than anything.

"I'll text you the details," he says and releases me.

My mouth hangs open, and I can't even form words. My skin is still tingling, waiting for him to kiss me, but he's already heading toward the door.

I'm never the girl at a loss for words.

Never.

But I'm standing in my bedroom, unable to move like a moron. I hate the way Leo Conti plays with my emotions and how my body betrays me every time he's around.

Tomorrow night, I will not be a pawn.

"WHY DO you keep looking at your phone?" Angelo asks.

I look up, not even realizing how often I've come back to the counter just to see if Leo texted me about our date.

"No reason," I say and smile, hoping he'll drop the subject.

"You never look at your phone at work," he tells me, pointing out the obvious and never letting anyone's bullshit slide. "And that smile—" he points at me and drops his chin "—is bullshit."

"Fine. If you must know, I'm waiting for a call."

"Must be pretty important."

"It's not, Betty," I tease him.

He's being nosy as fuck, just like our mom. Angelo's usually the one to mind his own business, but tonight he's a little too interested for my liking.

He pushes five beers in front of me. "Take these to table five." When I don't move right away, he says, "Please."

"Only because you asked nicely." I quickly glance down at the blank phone screen before grabbing the beers and hustling toward table five.

"Sweetheart, settle a bet," one of the men says as I set the beers down at their table. I let the little nickname slide because one, he's a paying customer, and two, I've been called worse.

I tilt my head and place my hands on my hips. They're so intoxicated, I'm sure their pressing question is going to be a doozy. "Shoot," I tell him with a quick nod.

"Can we be crass?" the guy closest to me asks, and I'm honestly impressed he uses such a big word.

"Sure."

"Okay, so... You've been dating a guy for a month, and it's finally the big day you two are going to do it." The guys around the table are all giggling like schoolgirls except one, the guy I assume they're all making fun of with this little question. "You're about to get busy, he drops his drawers, and his penis is so small it's almost an innie... What do you do?"

I honestly feel bad for the guy. I don't know what's worse—having the world's tiniest penis, or his friends knowing about it.

"He better be damn good with his tongue," I say.

The looks on their faces are priceless.

"So, you wouldn't end the relationship?" another guy asks.

I shake my head. "Let's face it, boys. Someday, all your dicks won't work and will be useless anyway, but a tongue is forever." I smirk as their mouths hang open.

I turn my back and head toward the bar, but I stop dead when I see Angelo staring at my glowing phone.

Oh no. Shit.

I walk faster, and any sense of victory from moments ago is gone. I quickly snatch my phone off the bar as soon as I can.

"So, who's *The Best You'll Ever Have*?"

I stare at my phone, seeing the funny little name he must've put in my contacts when I was sleeping or you know...passed out.

"We're just friends." I slide my finger across the screen, opening the entire message, thankful Angelo could only see the nickname.

I'm typing out a reply when Michelle walks up to us and looks over my shoulder. "Who are you texting?" she asks, being just as nosy as my brother.

"The best she'll ever have," Angelo tells her.

I glare at him. "Don't start," I warn.

"Daphne, you can't be serious," Michelle says because she knows exactly who we're talking about.

"You know him?" Angelo raises an eyebrow, getting all intense.

I turn to her and narrow my eyes. "Shut your mouth, Michelle," I whisper.

"No." Michelle smiles at Angelo and shakes her head. "I don't know him, know him."

I'm ready to reach out and wrap my fingers around her neck, strangling the life out of her and the ability to rat me out. She's my best friend and is always supposed to have my back, even when I'm fucking everything up.

"He's just some guy we met," Michelle says, covering for me and therefore saving her own life.

Angelo isn't buying what she's selling, but he doesn't have time to argue because a customer on the other end of the bar is waving him down. One of his female regulars who only wants him.

Michelle snatches the phone from my hand. "You can't be serious with this shit. You know how dangerous he is?"

I grab the phone back before stuffing it into my back pocket to avoid anything else being seen. "He said one date and he'd leave me alone," I tell her.

"A man like Leo doesn't do just one date, Daphne."

"How would you know?"

"I heard about him." She raises an eyebrow as her lips flatten.

"Heard what?"

"I'm just warning you now he's not someone you could be involved with." She pauses and rubs the back of her neck, glancing around to make sure no one's listening. "There's your father. Plus, I heard Leo doesn't like to give up control and can be a complete dick."

"It's only one date. What could go wrong?"

Michelle rolls her eyes and glances up toward the ceiling. "Everything."

CHAPTER SIX

DAPHNE

Leo's text was cryptic. He simply said to be ready at six and wear a dress with heels. He didn't drop a clue as to where he's taking me even though I asked many times. He only sent back a quick reply that stated, "You'll see," and left it at that.

When I make my way downstairs and open the door to my building, I expect to see Leo, but he's not here. Instead, there's a man dressed in a black suit with dark sunglasses, and a fancy car parked at the curb.

"Good evening, ma'am," he says, dipping his head slightly.

I peer to the left and then to the right, waiting for Leo to pop out of somewhere and yell surprise.

"Mr. Conti is waiting for you at your destination."

"Where are we going?" I ask with a shaky voice as I pull the door closed behind me and wonder if I'm walking to my death.

I'm headed off to God knows where. Maybe it's a trap. Anything's possible with my father now out of prison. Leo could very well be kidnapping me to hand me over to his father in some crazy-ass Chicago mafia coup d'état.

"I'm under strict orders not to reveal a single detail." The driver walks ahead of me, and I follow like a lamb stupidly heading to slaughter.

"Wait." I stop and grab my phone out of my purse. I shoot Leo a text, asking what the fuck he's thinking sending a strange man to my door when I'm already apprehensive about going out on this date to begin with.

The man folds his hands in front of his chest, watching me, not the least bit amused.

Leo: Just get in the car, Daphne.

Easy for him to say.

He's the one in the know, while I'm clueless and supposed to trust a man I barely know.

Sure, he's hot as hell, but beyond that, I only know our fathers hate each other.

I punch in a quick reply, trying to take deep breaths before I hyperventilate.

Me: You could be kidnapping me.

There's a brief pause before he starts typing something back.

Leo: I could've done that when you were passed out. Just get in the car. It's a surprise.

Me: I hate surprises. They don't mesh well in my world.

The driver's phone rings, and he turns his back to me before answering the call. "Yes, sir," he says quietly. "I understand."

I tap my foot, waiting for someone to give me a straight answer or I'm turning around and calling off the big date. "Well?" I say as soon as he faces me again.

"Mr. Conti has instructed me to tell you we're going to the airport. But beyond that, he'd like to keep it a surprise."

"The airport?" I nearly choke.

"Ma'am, Mr. Conti has chartered a private plane for the evening. Now, if you'll please." He motions toward the car. "I don't like to keep him waiting."

"I'm sure you don't." I walk past the super stiff driver and head toward the car.

He rushes in front of me, grabbing the handle before I can and opening the back door. "Ma'am." He pauses and straightens, somehow looking even stiffer than before.

I slide into the back seat and look around the sleek, black-leather interior, kind of impressed with the lengths Leo's going to for our date.

The driver gets in and doesn't say a word as he pulls away from the curb. I stare out the tinted windows, wondering if I'll ever make it back home again and know I have to tell someone where I'm going just in case.

Me: Leo's taking me on a plane ride. Private jet. If I don't come back, he did it!

Michelle's going to have something to say about the unplanned trip. She was already pissed I was going out with Leo, but now that I'm taking a plane ride to God knows where, she'll be livid.

So instead of reading her text messages chastising me for being an idiot, I tuck my phone back into my purse and enjoy the view from the seclusion of the back seat of the luxury sedan.

My hands are practically shaking as we pull into the airport on the outskirts of town. The sun's setting behind the trees, splashing the sky with vibrant yellows and stunning oranges like something out of a painting. Leo's standing at the base of the stairway, looking just as handsome as ever in another expensive suit. There's no smile on his face until the driver opens the door and I step outside.

"You made it." He walks toward me. "Decided I wasn't going to ransom you off or kill you?"

I laugh nervously, knowing I had been ridiculous. "I'm trusting you, Leo." I peer up into his deep, rich eyes. "Don't break that trust. I don't give it easily."

Leo places his hands on my upper arms, and the

72

spark I felt before zaps me again. "I promise to have you back before the sun rises and in perfect condition."

I wouldn't mind a little imperfection if it included a round in the sack with Leo as a parting gift, of course. But then I remember having sex with him will only complicate matters even more than they already are, and I decide I will not sleep with Leo Conti.

I place my palm flat against his chest, feeling his heart beating out of control just like mine. "Something has been bothering me." I keep my eyes locked with his. "I need to know one thing before I get on the plane with you."

"Ask me anything. I have nothing to hide." He doesn't blink.

I glance toward the waiting jet and clear my throat. "My brother's wedding."

Leo nods, bringing my attention back to him.

"Why were you there? I know you weren't invited."

He slides his palms up and down my arms, stirring the lust seated deep in my belly. "It's a long story. Why don't we get on board, and I'll tell you everything? We have an hour before we land."

"Not good enough," I tell him, but I don't back away. My mind is telling me to run, but my body's not listening.

Leo's palm slides down my arm before covering my hand resting on his chest. "I was in the hotel and just stopped in. I never meant to talk to anyone or be seen. I promise to tell you whatever you want to know once we're on the plane, but we're going to be late."

"Late?"

"For our dinner reservations."

"Which are where?"

I know I'm being difficult and I'm fishing, but damn it, surprises have never been my thing. I've had too many in life, especially when it comes to my father. I like to know what I'm walking into before I'm smacked in the face with reality.

"Nashville," he says finally. "Figure there's no chance of the old guidos seeing us there."

"We could've just gone to the Little Village for some margaritas."

Leo shakes his head and sighs. "Their reach is everywhere in Chicago, even with the Mexican cartel."

I open my mouth to say something, but nothing comes out. Leo's been dropping information left and right when I'm with him, and it's all news to me. I figured my father's business was far-reaching, but I never really thought about how vast his network could possibly be.

Leo holds my chin between his fingers. "I promise you won't regret tonight."

I stare into his eyes, looking for any reason not to go. "Okay," I say when I don't find any.

Leo leans forward, still holding my chin, our eyes locked. "I promise you'll have a good time," he says softly with his lips practically touching mine.

My breathing slows, and time almost seems to stop as he hovers just out of reach. His brown eyes darken, and the way he stares at me leaves me nothing short of needy.

"Not here," he whispers before backing away.

My hand falls from his chest, and I'm left gasping for air, trying to recover from the nearness of him.

I've never felt this way with anyone.

No one except Leo Conti.

I think back to the moment I met him up until now. I haven't stopped craving his touch, his kiss, his everything.

His hand is on the small of my back as we walk on to the plane. He greets the pilot, introducing me, but leaving my last name out of the entire brief conversation.

There's just the three of us for the short flight. A bottle of chilled champagne is waiting near the leather sofa that runs down one side of the plane.

Leo motions for me to sit before he pours two glasses. "Buckle up," he says with a smirk as the plane starts to taxi down the runway. "It may be a bumpy ride."

No truer words have ever been spoken. There's nothing smooth about the storm that's brewing inside me and the hurricane barreling our way if I don't put an end to whatever this is before we touch down again in Chicago.

The takeoff isn't as smooth as I'd hoped or am used

to in a commercial airplane. I've never been fond of flying, and being in a small private plane doesn't alleviate the anxiety that has settled deep in my core.

After I quickly polish off the first glass of champagne, I pour myself another and pray it will be enough to calm me down.

Leo places his hand on my knee, which hasn't stopped shaking since the moment the plane lifted off the ground. "Are you okay?"

I smile nervously and wave the champagne flute between us, almost spilling the contents in his lap. "I'm great. Fine. Never been better," I blurt out, making it quite obvious I'm a hot mess.

He squeezes my knee. I take a deep breath, trying to focus on my breathing along with his deep, penetrating gaze instead of the fact that we're high in the air.

He turns on the couch next to me, bringing his knee against mine, connecting our bodies once again. "You asked why I was at the wedding." He pauses as he sets his champagne flute on the table at his side. "For weeks, I'd heard rumors your father was being released from prison. When I saw the last name for the wedding party in the grand ballroom, I thought I'd stop in and see if he was there."

My entire body rocks backward. "You were stalking us?"

"No, no. It's not like that."

I raise an eyebrow and cross my arms, carefully

holding the champagne flute in front of me. "It sounds exactly like that."

"I'm like you, Daphne. I have nothing to do with my father's business, but somehow, his world bleeds into mine. Especially when one of his enemies is after him. We both know the bloody histories of our fathers' business endeavors."

I nod, but I'm not quite sure I have a firm grasp on it like Leo does.

"I needed to see with my own eyes if Santino Gallo was really out, walking the streets again."

"You think my father would order a hit on yours?"

"I have no doubt my father would order one on your father if he deemed it necessary. Why would your father be any different? Hell, they'd probably kill us and not even blink."

I open my mouth to speak and close it again. I'm in complete and utter shock. None of us is involved in my father's hustle. Not in any way are we even remotely tied to his business dealings besides the simple fact that we were born.

"That's ridiculous," I tell him.

Leo moves even closer. "I needed to know if your father was released and if I had to increase the security around my sisters and myself. We're not part of their world, but it's very easy for us to become casualties."

I think back to the wedding, the moment I tripped, and how Leo caught me. "You swear you didn't know who I was when I left the ballroom with you?"

He holds his hands up. "I didn't know at first. I never went to the wedding with the intention of sleeping with Santino's daughter. After you fell into my arms, I wanted to talk to you."

"When you asked me to go somewhere quiet, you were going to fuck me, weren't you?" I'm straightforward with my questioning.

His hand is back on my knee, stroking the spot that makes my belly tighten. "There was a spark between us from the moment I touched you, Daphne. I've never felt that with another person. Maybe it's your fiery mouth or your beautiful lips, but I can't stop myself from wanting you. Couldn't keep myself from taking you home that night and thinking about you nonstop since the moment you walked out of my place, leaving your scent in my bed and turning my world upside down."

I swallow roughly, knowing exactly what he's talking about. From the moment I first heard his voice, my body has responded to him in every way. Even his touch sends goose bumps across my skin. I should hate him. I should stay away, but Leo makes that impossible, and my body's reaction isn't helping.

"Our fathers are enemies. You said it yourself, neither would think twice about offing one of us. Normal people don't hop on private planes to fly to a different state to stay under the radar for a date. There's so much wrong with this, Leo. So much is fucked up about the entire situation."

Leo's grip tightens on my leg. "And yet, somehow, there's so much that's right. Tell me you don't feel it."

God, I want to tell him he's wrong and to go to hell, but I can't seem to get the words out of my mouth. I'm having trouble even thinking. Leo's too close, his skin on mine, and the plane's vibrating, reminding me we're high in the air.

Leo Conti could very well be my undoing.

CHAPTER SEVEN

LEO

Up until the plane ride, I hadn't given Daphne one good reason to think I was an honorable man or trustworthy in any way.

Hell, I didn't even bother to correct her when she thought we'd had sex. It was a sleazeball move, but I liked her thinking we'd done more than actually sleep together.

Tonight, I'd reserved the chef's table at the fanciest and most exclusive steakhouse in Nashville. Dining in the kitchen gave us more privacy, and I didn't want her looking over her shoulder most of the night instead of keeping her eyes on me.

Daphne fidgets, touching the silverware on both sides of her plate as soon as we sit down. "This is impressive."

"Nothing but the best," I tell her, pouring the champagne I selected earlier for this special occasion.

"You really shouldn't have gone to all this trouble," she says as she takes the champagne flute from my hand. "It's beautiful, but I'm really a simple girl."

"There's nothing simple about you, Daphne."

She blushes and looks away before lifting the champagne to her lips.

"Leo, my dear friend," Martin, the chef and owner, says as he approaches our table.

"Martin, thank you for having us this evening on such short notice."

"Ah. Anything for you. Your lady is quite beautiful." He smiles at Daphne, no doubt just as struck by her beauty as I am. Daphne's blush only deepens as Martin continues to talk. "But you've always been a lucky bastard."

"I've never been as lucky as I am tonight." I wink at Daphne, wanting her to know exactly how I feel.

"I have to get back to work, but your first course will be ready shortly."

"Thank you," Daphne says to Martin with the sweetest smile.

"It is entirely my pleasure, madam." He tips his

head, drinking her in in much the same way most men do when they cross her path.

"He seems really nice," Daphne says, watching over my shoulder as Martin is no doubt putting on a show. "Have you known him long?"

"For a few years. We used to work together before he decided to open this restaurant. I helped him get it off the ground, becoming part owner until he was able to buy me out."

"Well, that was nice of you."

"It was purely a business decision," I tell her, but I would've done anything for Martin. He helped me launch my hotel in Nashville, ensuring it was a success in an already flooded market.

"I find that hard to believe," she says, smiling at me over the rim of her champagne flute.

"I'm a good guy, Daphne." I feel like I'm pleading my case, trying to get her to think of me as someone other than Mario's son.

"I realize that now."

"Can I ask you something?" I stare across the table at the most beautiful woman I've ever seen. "What makes you tick?"

She leans forward, holding the champagne flute in one hand and looking way more delicious than anything Martin could ever serve. "My family and my business."

My answer would be the same. But someday, I'd like to have my own family. As the years roll by, I realize I'm not getting any younger, and the need to settle down becomes stronger and more urgent.

I lean across the table and brush a few strands of hair away from her eyes, but my touch lingers. "What brings you pleasure?"

The candlelight flickers across her face as her eyes darken, and she moves into my touch. "Right now, you do," she admits. "And you?"

"Being with you."

"We shouldn't do this," she whispers.

"Do what? We're only talking." I feel absolutely no guilt for how I feel or what we're doing.

I don't care about our families, our friends, or any repercussions that could come out of our evening together.

"We're doing more than talking, Leo," she says softly, blinking slowly and seducing me even more.

Martin clears his throat, interrupting the moment we were just having. "Can I just say you two make a gorgeous couple? Never have I seen two people more perfect for each other."

Daphne and I exchange a look over the table before I reply. "Thank you, Martin. We don't want to get ahead of ourselves. This is our first date."

Martin sets down the plates he's been holding. "I'm so sorry. I misspoke. I never would've guessed this is your first date."

"It's fine." Daphne smiles easily. "It doesn't feel like our first date either."

"Well, enjoy the Oysters Rockefeller. They're the house specialty and an aphrodisiac." He winks before leaving us alone again.

She relaxes back into her seat and stares at me across the table. "You're not what I expected. Not at all."

I raise an eyebrow. "Is that good or bad?"

"Well, I figured you were an asshole."

"Oh." I laugh. "I am."

"Not really."

"No. I really am, but maybe you're too blinded by your feelings for me to see it."

Daphne smirks. "Hardly," she whispers.

WE'RE HALFWAY BACK to Chicago, and I know my time is running out to get her to agree to another date. Even though I asked her for only one, I sure as hell want more.

"I like you, Daphne. I don't care what your last name is. I don't care who your father is or who my father is. I don't care that it's dangerous to be around you. I don't care that if your father finds out, he'll probably end my life before I can blink. All I care about is you. The way your skin feels against mine. The way your breathing changes when I touch you. I want all of it. I'm not ready to walk away without finding out what this is between us."

"It's a lot for me to process," she says, totally not going where I wanted after professing what's happening in my head.

Daphne's been staring at me all night. Practically undressing me with her eyes like she did the night I met her. Her lips may have said one thing, but her body has always portrayed the opposite.

The straight line across Daphne's top lip dips. "Leo," she whispers and shakes her head as she sits next to me on the plane. "Tonight was nice, but we could never work."

"Why? Give me one good reason." I'm being pushy, but nothing is ever gained without being relentless.

"Um." She laughs softly. "The possibility of one of us dying is a pretty damn good reason, you know?" She shrugs with a crooked smile.

"We're all going to die someday, Daphne, but it's how we choose to live that's most important."

She stares at me for a minute, blinking with her lips parted. I can't tell if my statement was a home run or the proverbial nail in my coffin of anything possibly happening between us.

"Did we at least kiss that night?" she asks.

I cover my mouth to hide my smile. This woman has me all kinds of crazy, and I can't seem to stop myself from wanting more. "You don't remember anything?"

Daphne shakes her head. "Not really."

"Nothing?" I ask again in complete shock.

"Not a minute after the reception," she tells me. "I think I would've remembered things if they were that earth-shattering or life-altering, but I have nothing. There's not even a hint of a memory."

I slide closer, wanting to be near her. "We didn't even kiss. But I want to kiss you," I tell her, needing to touch her lips more than anything in the world. "I'm going to kiss you."

Her eyes widen, but she doesn't pull away or protest. I place my fingers under her chin, holding her eyes to mine.

"If there's no spark, no connection, and you feel nothing, we'll call this quits. You can walk off this plane, and you'll never hear from me again. But," I say and pause, leaning forward a little more and bringing my face closer to hers. "If you feel what I do, we see what happens. We owe ourselves that much."

She doesn't say anything as she stares deep into my eyes. Daphne's barely breathing, and the air around us is thick and crackling with lust.

Her gaze drops to my lips as I move forward. I'm hungry for her. This girl has my body, mind, and soul all tied up in knots. She's like some great cosmic joke, making me fall for the one girl in the entire city of Chicago I shouldn't be falling for.

I slide my hand up her cheek, cupping her face in my palm as I press my lips to her soft, inviting mouth. The same electric shocks I felt before vibrate

CHELLE BLISS

throughout my system as our bodies connect and our breathing becomes synchronized. She moves into my touch, her body craving the kiss as much as my own.

I want her. I want her more than I've ever wanted anything or anyone in my entire life. I'm used to getting what I want, but Daphne Gallo isn't going to be an easy conquest. She's going to fight me tooth and nail, and I'll use any weapons necessary to win.

My fingers press into the nape of her neck, tipping her head back and allowing me to kiss her deeper and harder than before. She moans softly, sending the electric sparks scattering across my nerves, shocking my heart out of rhythm.

Sliding my other arm around her back, I pull her closer, wanting to feel her body against mine. As if on cue, she crawls into my lap, settling her warm, lush pussy against my agonizingly stiff cock. She digs her fingers in my hair, kissing me back with more fervor and passion than she did the night we met.

She feels. She can't deny what this is. The lust. The passion. The want. The need. It's there. It's undeniable. It's not love. It's not caring. It's sexual and inescapable for both of us.

She tips her head back, giving me full access to her neck. I slide my lips down her jaw, following a path to her pulse. Her heart's pounding feverishly, matching my own. I tangle my fingers in her hair, holding her in this position so I can feast on her flesh.

The plane drops, and Daphne gasps, stilling in my

arms. "We're safe, *bella*," I whisper against her skin before distracting her with my touch. "I got you."

When I bite down gently on the soft spot near her shoulder, she relaxes in my arms and lets out a soft moan. She grinds against me, rocking her core across my cock. I'm a goner. Any resistance I have is quickly slipping, making it impossible for me to go slow.

"I want you. I need you," I admit, knowing full well the explosive pleasure our bodies produce together. I'm not the type of man to admit such things. Especially not so early and with an unknown outcome. But Daphne Gallo does that to me. She makes me different from my usual self. She makes me...better.

Her fingers fall from my hair and are at the buckle of my belt, working quickly to release the metal prong, and I'm silently thanking the man above for letting her feel the spark too.

I release her hair, sliding my hands down her sides until I find the hem of her dress. Her skin's soft and warm, calling me to touch every inch and lose myself in her completely as our mouths fuse together again.

She pulls at my zipper, yanking the metal down easily and exposing the head of my cock. Her fingernail brushes against the tip, and I'm momentarily breathless. When she reaches inside, wrapping her silky fingers around my hard shaft, I almost lose it.

I need to be inside her. I need to feel her around me more than I need the air I breathe. I shove her dress upward, exposing her bare pussy, and dig my fingers into the tender flesh of her ass. She scoots forward, placing her wetness against my hardness.

She lifts her bottom, one hand on my shoulder, and stares at me. With my cock in her hand, she says, "I feel it too, and I'm about to fuck it out of my system."

I don't argue.

I'm up for the challenge.

I'm about to fuck her so good, she'll be begging for my cock again. This isn't our goodbye. I refuse to let her throw me away, making me nothing more than a warm body and a hard cock with an expiration date.

Daphne drops down on my dick, impaling herself on my entire length as she digs her fingernails into the skin underneath my dress shirt.

The pain and pleasure mix has my head spinning and my ability to breathe almost nonexistent. I don't want this fast. I want her slow. I want to feel every inch inside her and for her to feel me buried deep within her for days.

I grip her hips, slowing the pace as I swivel my hips, making sure to hit every pleasurable spot inside her. Her head tips back as she moans, giving up control to me. Rocking into her, I thrust my hips upward as I pull her downward, slamming our bodies together in unison.

She cries out, her hand still on my shoulder, nails digging into me, and I'm fucking loving every moment of this. Daphne's brown hair cascades down her back, sweeping against my pants as she tethers me to her with her grip.

"You feel that?" I ask as I pummel her slick pussy with my entire cock.

She moans, not giving me the answer I want verbally, but her body convulses as I speak.

"Do you feel the way I want you? The way I need you?" My voice is rough and my breathing even more ragged than before. "Look at me," I order her, wanting the connection deeper than just the flesh.

Her dark brown eyes connect with mine, and something snaps. I pull her face to mine, crashing my lips against hers as I pick up the pace, thrusting my cock deeper and harder than before. I'm chasing the high only Daphne Gallo gives me.

Her insides constrict around me, sucking me deeper, stealing my breath. Her body's pulling out the orgasm I'm not ready to give. I want more of this. I want more of her.

She bucks against me and pushes my hands away, bucking and bouncing on my dick as her tongue dances with mine.

I'm lost.

I'm a goner.

I'm completely addicted to Daphne Gallo, and I've never been so completely fucked in my entire life.

CHAPTER EIGHT

DAPHNE

"WHAT'S THAT?" Michelle moves my collar aside and gasps. "Did Leo do that again?"

I slap her hand away and cover the spot I thought I had concealed. "I fell," I blurt out, but we both know it's bullshit.

That bastard. He left a bruise on my neck where he bit me on the plane as I rode him through multiple orgasms. I no longer regret the claw marks I no doubt left on his shoulder either. I now realize he's quite fond of leaving a mark somewhere on my body, and not in a discreet place, which I'm sure is part of his master plan.

Michelle grabs the side of her head and grunts. "Are you fucking stupid, or do you have a death wish?"

At this point, I'm thinking a little bit of both. Why else would I be drawn back to Leo...repeatedly?

Angelo walks behind the bar and narrows his eyes, zeroing in on the hickey on my neck.

"Lower your voice." I motion toward my brother with my chin, not wanting him to hear a word of our conversation.

She glances at Angelo and smiles like she's covering our tracks and totally failing. "Answer the question." She doesn't even move her lips when she speaks.

"I ended things," I tell her.

At least, that's what I told him when I kissed him goodbye as we stood outside his plane on the runway. Even though we fucked like rabbits and he quite possibly may have given me the best orgasms of my life, I wasn't sure I could see him again.

There is no future for us.

How could there be?

Our families are enemies, and by extension, so are we.

Michelle crosses her arms over her chest, cocking her head to the side and giving me a look. "Are you sure?"

"Of course," I scoff and wave my hand in the air. "Totally."

She narrows her gaze. "He may be on the up-and-up, but we both know his father isn't."

"Neither is mine," I remind her, but she knows my father just as well as I do.

Michelle grew up in the life too. Her father worked for mine until he passed away five years ago in a tragic car accident. She wondered for a long time if it was a hit, but so far, we haven't found any evidence. My father swears there was no war going on and everything that happened to Eddie, Michelle's dad, was accidental.

She glances up at the ceiling. "Is it really over between you two, or are you bullshitting me?"

"Yes. It's really over," I say, but I don't even convince myself, and I know Michelle doesn't buy it either.

"So, it was that good, wasn't it?"

"What was?" I play stupid.

"The sex." She shakes her head, annoyed with me. "You said he had a perfect penis and the best body you'd ever seen."

"Girl." I let out a loud sigh. "He was the best ever."

"Toe-curling?" The corner of her mouth ticks up.

We've always been honest with each other and never hid anything before... Why start now?

"Everything curling. I'm in trouble here, Michelle. Real trouble."

"Daphne, your phone is vibrating across the bar,"

Johnny says as he lifts my cell phone up and stares at the screen. "Who's The Best You'll Ever Have?"

"Oh fuck," I mutter and leave Michelle behind, marching straight to Johnny and plucking my phone from his grip.

Angelo looks at me, and I can see the questions already swirling around in his head. "Who you seein', Daphne?" Angelo finally asks as I jam my phone into my purse underneath the bar. "It's not the first time he's called."

I don't turn around, keeping my back to him because it's easier to lie when I don't have to face him. "No one."

The words are almost truthful. I'm not seeing Leo. Well, not anymore, at least. We aren't a thing. We fucked. Okay, we fucked a few times, but that doesn't make us a *thing*.

"You were MIA last night, and now you show up with a hickey on your neck again," he says.

"Fuck," I whisper and close my eyes, pretending to dig in my purse for something that's not there. "I fell down. That's what the bruise is from. It's not a hickey, jagoff."

"So, you fell and hit your neck?" His voice rises on the last word.

I lift my face to find Michelle staring at me, twisting her lips as she tries to hide her laughter. I give her a look that's nothing short of deadly. "Something like that." I stand, finally turning toward my brother and somehow keeping a straight face. "Anyway, I'm fine."

"And the phone call?" He raises an eyebrow.

"Just some random dude."

Angelo looks to Michelle and she nods, but there's no smile on her face. She's the lamest liar on the planet. Although she'd be the first person at my side to fuck shit up, she'd also be the first one singing to the cops and confessing all our crimes, especially if Angelo were the detective. She's always had a thing for him, even though she tries to hide it. I'm not stupid or blind.

"Yeah. He's no one, really," Michelle says with the fakest laugh I've ever heard.

Angelo doesn't say anything more, but his eyes are still on me. There's no way in hell I'm telling him anything more than he needs to know. And right now, he doesn't need to know about Leo.

I start to walk away, satisfied that the conversation's over, when Angelo says, "Billy saw you at the little airport outside of town last night."

I freeze mid-stride with one leg in the air, waiting for the proverbial other shoe to drop. My eyes are wide and locked on Michelle, and she looks just as horrified as me.

That fucker has been leading me on, knowing full well I was with someone, but playing stupid, trying to get me to crack. But I'm a pro. Growing up Gallo has taught me a thing or two...evasion being one of those skills.

"He said you were with some guy getting on a private jet last night. Billy said the guy looked familiar, but he couldn't place his face. Well, not yet, at least. Did you take a little trip, sis? Maybe with the Best You'll Ever Have."

I spin around on one heel like I'm a freaking ballerina and stare down my brother. "I don't have to tell you anything. Mind your own business." He dips his head, and the corner of his mouth tips upward, making me angrier. "I don't ask you who you're screwing, and you don't get to ask me, big brother."

I give Michelle a smile, feeling mighty impressed with myself and my ability to hold it together even under Angelo's penetrating gaze. Well, to be fair, my back was to him most of the time, but still.

"I don't care who you're with, Daphne. Just be careful and be smart."

Careful—I had been careful. Leo was careful because he knew there were eyes on us. Smart. That was something entirely different. If I were smart, I wouldn't have agreed to the one date, and I most definitely wouldn't have banged him, officially becoming a member of the mile-high club.

I stalk back to the bar, grabbing my purse and phone from under the countertop. "I'm always smart, Angelo. Always," I lie.

I march out of the room, making my exit, and head to the alley. I'm already listening to Leo's voice mail when the door slams behind me.

Daphne. I can't stop thinking about you. You said goodbye, but I know you didn't mean it. I'll be at your place tonight. Don't shoot me.

I can't wipe the smile off my face, but then I remember the possibility of one of us winding up dead.

Me: It's too dangerous. Someone saw us at the airport.

I tap my foot, waiting for him to text me back, but when nothing comes, I take a step back inside. I'm not even three feet down the hallway when my phone finally rings.

"What do you mean someone saw us?" I can hear the worry in Leo's voice.

"One of my brother's friends works at the airport. He ratted on me."

"Fuck," he hisses.

"I don't think we should see each other again, Leo. It's too dangerous. You were careful, and someone still saw us."

"Do they know who I am?"

"Since the guy works at the airport, I'm sure he can figure it out."

"The plane's registered in the company name."

"And which company would that be?"

He still hasn't told me much about his work besides the fact that he's in no way involved with his father's business. I wasn't going to push the subject, but since he brought the topic up, I think, what the hell. Why not?

"Excellence Hotels."

"Like *the* Excellence Hotels?"

My brother's wedding was at the Excellence. Now, the reason for Leo to be at the hotel made perfect sense and how he knew which couple was celebrating in the grand ballroom that evening too.

He wasn't stalking my family, after all.

"Yes," he replies.

"Are you, like, the CEO or something?"

"I own the hotel chain, Daphne."

My mouth hangs open. I knew Leo was wealthy, I knew Leo had class, but never did I think he was the owner of one of the biggest and most elite hotel chains in the country.

"Well, okay," I say, still in shock from the truth bomb he just dropped on me. "We still shouldn't see each other again. When I said goodbye, I meant it."

"We'll talk about it tonight," he says and hangs up.

I gawk at my phone in disbelief.

He hung up on me.

Fucking Leo Conti just hit end on our conversation without letting me get another word out, and I had plenty to say.

"Are you working, or are you going to chitchat all day?" Angelo asks, scaring the living hell out of me.

"Jesus," I mutter, grabbing my chest. "I'm coming."

Angelo stares at me. He knows something's up. I just hope he doesn't find out who I've been seeing because I know he'd have something to say about it. He hates my father's business as much as I do.

I jam my phone into my back pocket and walk toward the bar, brushing against his shoulder as I pass by.

I'm busy pulling down the new bottles for tonight's service when my mom pushes through the front door, carrying an old bicycle frame in her arms with the biggest smile on her face.

"Look at this beauty." She lifts the rusty heap higher when she approaches us.

"It's... It's..." I don't know what to say to her. I know she wants to hear how wonderful the hunk of junk is, but I just can't seem to find the right words. It's a rusty mess, but to her, it's a work of art.

"It's great, Ma," Angelo says quickly, saving me before I utter something I know I'll regret.

Her smile grows larger as she rests the frame on the floor. "I know exactly what I'm going to make, too."

My mother has become interested in reclamation art or, as I call it, junk. When my father was sent away to prison, Ma needed to find a hobby to pass the time, and why she didn't pick up crocheting or knitting, I'll never understand.

Instead, she takes what other people throw out and repurposes it to create a "work of art"—her words, not mine—that no one ever wants to buy.

I feign interest because well...she's my mom, and I

can't be disrespectful. "What?" I ask, but I don't really care to know the answer.

She holds the frame with one hand and takes a step back, staring at the rusting disaster. "Picture this." She waves her hand between the frame and herself. "I'm going to use this as the base for a coffee table. Maybe I'll use glass for the tabletop. Wouldn't that be fabulous?"

"Sounds great, Ma," Angelo says, always the one to kiss my mother's ass.

"Ass-kisser," I mouth, rolling my eyes so only he can see.

"Daphne wants it for her living room," he tells her with a shitty smirk. "She's been talking about getting a new coffee table for a long time."

My mom starts to clap, excited at the thought of me finally displaying a piece of her work in my place. "It's serendipity," she chirps.

With my back still to my mother, I glare at Angelo and flip him off. "I'll get you back," I mutter quietly before turning to face my mother. "I'd love to have it, Ma, but I hate glass. Can you at least make the top metal or wood?"

Part of me is hoping I'll kill her vision and she'll decide to keep the table for herself, but I should've known that wasn't my mother's way.

"Sure, honey. Anything you want." She's so happy I almost feel guilty that I want a solid top to hide the fact that there will be a piece of junk holding the entire thing up. "I'm going to go out back and start working on it." She grabs the bike frame, and before either of us can say another word, she scurries toward the hallway to her "art studio" in an abandoned garage behind the bar.

"That's going to look amazing in your place, Daph." Angelo laughs.

"You're an asshole!" I yell as he walks toward the other end of the bar, avoiding the dagger I'm pretending to throw his way.

CHAPTER NINE

LEO

I'M WALKING through the lobby on my way to see Daphne when I spot my father sitting at the hotel bar, sipping on a glass of brandy. He never comes here. Not unless he wants something.

We've always had an agreement. He keeps his business out of my hotels, and I try to ignore the fact that he's a criminal.

"Hey, Pop," I say, motioning to the bartender to pour me a drink because I have a feeling I'm going to need it. "What brings you here tonight?"

"I heard you were in the old neighborhood the

other night." He swishes the brandy around the inside of the glass, beating around the bush instead of coming right out and asking me what he really wants to know.

That's my father's way.

He'd always pry but pretend he wasn't actually fishing for information.

Tonight, my father looks tired. The lines near the corners of his eyes seem deeper than the last time I saw him. There're more gray streaks running through his perfectly placed black hair. Time is catching up with a man who has seemed invincible my entire life.

"I was," I tell him, sliding the whiskey in front of me as soon as the bartender sets the glass down.

"It's not safe for you there." My father glances across his shoulder at me. "I thought you were smarter than that, Leo."

"I have nothing to do with your business, Pop."

His brown eyes narrow. "You're my son. Whether you like it or not, you're a target because you're my blood."

I take a sip of whiskey, listening to him go on and on about the danger I put myself in by going into enemy territory. I let him say his piece without argument because there's no reasoning with the man.

"I forbid you to go there again," he tells me like I'm a little kid and, somehow, he's still in charge of my life.

I lean back and stare at my father, wondering if he's high on a power trip or growing senile. "I'm a grown man. You no longer get to tell me where I can and can't go in the city."

"The Gallos are dangerous, my son. Santino is out of prison now, and I'm sure there will be a power play for him to regain some of the territory he lost in his absence."

"Maybe he's done with the hustle and is a changed man after prison."

My father laughs cynically. "There's no such thing. Prison only makes someone harder." He pauses for a moment as he takes a sip of brandy before continuing. "And a better criminal."

My father should know. He's spent his fair share of time behind bars. Mostly when I was younger because he was a hothead, craving the spotlight and trying to live out his *Scarface* fantasies.

"If something happens to me, the blood will be on your hands. I'm not part of your business and won't let your world dictate my life."

His stare turns colder. "If someone touches you, a war will break out. You are my child no matter how old you are, Leo. I will always try to protect you."

"Maybe it's time to retire, Pop. Ever think of that? Live a normal life away from the violence and without having to look over your shoulder constantly."

He cracks a smile. "There's no other life for me. Since your mother died," he pauses and does the sign of the cross, "God rest her soul, there's no reason for me to quit."

My chest tightens. "Then we'll have to agree to disagree."

He places his hand on my arm, which is as close to affection as my father can seem to muster with me. "Nothing good can come of you going there."

He's wrong about that. If he knew I was meeting with Daphne Gallo, he'd literally shit a brick before stroking out on the barstool next to me. But that's his problem, not mine.

I polish off my drink before rising to my feet. "I have to run, Pop. Anything else?"

He stares straight ahead, looking at the mirror behind the bar. "I don't like getting reports on your whereabouts, Leo."

"Then stop having me watched. Call your bulldogs off and remind them I'm not part of your business. I'm off-limits."

"Naïve," he mutters before I walk away.

I leave him sitting at the bar, nursing his drink and probably stewing over the fact that I don't seem to follow his advice.

My sisters are so much better than I am at listening to my father. They always have been. They're all pampered princesses, willing to take the dirty money to maintain the cushy and over-the-top lifestyles they grew accustomed to.

But I am nothing like them and never will be.

DAPHNE DOESN'T LOOK EXCITED to see me parked next to her Jeep behind the bar a little after midnight. "What are you doing here?"

"Get in."

She stares at me, blinking a few times, but she doesn't move. "You hang up on me, and now you're telling me to get in your car?"

"Yeah." I smirk.

No matter what she's saying, I know she's going to get in. She can act offended all she wants, but I know it's a front. The way she kissed me said everything I needed to know when it comes to Daphne Gallo.

"It's not safe for me to be here. So, get in the car so we can find someplace more private to talk."

Daphne glances around, looking into the darkness. I planted the seed, and that's all I needed to do before she marches around the back of my car and slides into the passenger seat.

"I'm here," she announces as she slams the door and then clears her throat. She folds her hands in her lap and stares out the front window, practically ignoring my presence.

I pull onto the street, heading toward my place where I know there's no one watching. "We've got to talk."

"I thought I said everything I needed to at the airport."

God, she's such a hard-ass. The woman doesn't

give in about anything, especially when it comes to her feelings.

We're sitting at a stoplight, and she still hasn't glanced in my direction. "You didn't mean it." Those words make her turn, and I could give two shits if it's out of anger. I have her attention now. "We both know that."

"I promised you a date. I gave you what you asked for, and I kept my word. We both know we'd never work. So, why force it?"

I don't answer her question as I pull away and maneuver through the streets of Chicago. I spend a few minutes planning my next move, my next words, and how I'm going to proceed with Daphne to get her to admit what she's feeling.

I don't need a profession of love, but knowing we're both on the same page physically would be nice. Everything else can be figured out later.

Since neither of us is involved in our father's businesses, there's nothing stopping us from seeing where this goes.

Once I pull into the secure underground parking below my building, I stop looking in the rearview mirror to see if we've been followed and finally relax. "Are you seeing someone else?" I ask as I park the car in my reserved spot and cut the engine.

"That would infer I'm seeing you, which I'm not. I'm seeing no one."

I shake my head and smile. I don't know if I've ever

met someone as maddening or stubborn as her. Why I enjoy her sharp tongue is beyond me. There're plenty of women who would enjoy being with me, and hell, they wouldn't put up this much of a fight.

Maybe that's why I like Daphne so much.

She isn't easy.

She doesn't give a rat's ass who I am or what I have, unlike some of the women I've had in my life.

"Come up for a bit, and then I'll take you home," I tell her as I open my car door, trying to at least get her into my place. Once I have her, I know she won't be so fast to leave.

She stares at me for a moment, not saying anything. I figure she's about ready to tell me to fuck off and take her ass home. Everything that's coming from her mouth is hinting in that direction, but she surprises me. "No kissing. Only talking. Got it?"

"Of course. I'll be a complete gentleman," I promise her.

She's out of the car before I am, stalking toward the bank of elevators just a few feet away. Her hips sway with each step, shaking her ass at me in a silent tease. She knows exactly what she's doing. She knows she drives me wild.

"Don't you miss the old neighborhood?" Her back is to me as she looks up, watching the floor numbers ticking by as the elevator descends.

"Sometimes."

Daphne and I grew up only a few blocks from each

other. Back then, our fathers weren't enemies and life was less complicated. I remember her brown hair, pulled tight in pigtails, blowing in the wind as she'd ride her bike down the street, terrorizing the other kids. She was a pistol then and hasn't mellowed with age.

She gives me the side-eye as she glances over her shoulder. "Why are you looking at me like that?"

"Just remembering you as a little girl." My smile widens. "You haven't changed all that much."

"That's funny," she says, turning back around as the elevator dings. She steps inside, walking all the way to the back before facing me again. "I can't seem to remember you."

"I remember plenty about you." I don't take my eyes off her. "I remember the pink bike you rode around the neighborhood, bullying half the kids to get your way."

"I loved that bike." Her eyebrows draw downward. "Why don't I remember you?"

"I'm older, and I didn't go to St. Catherine's."

"Ah. Wait. So you did know who I was at the wedding, then. I mean, we grew up with each other. How could you not know?"

"The last time I saw you, you were seven. You've changed a bit."

When shit went south between my father and hers, we moved out of the neighborhood and away from everyone and everything I ever loved. It wasn't until years later that I really understood why we'd had to move.

She grabs her breasts, lifting them higher and giving me a show in her V-neck T-shirt. "I know I didn't have these," she teases, knowing full well she's driving me mad and loving every second of the sweet torture she's inflicting.

I close my eyes, wishing the elevator moved a little faster or I lived on a lower floor. "Your mouth hasn't changed at all."

CHAPTER TEN

DAPHNE

Leo's penthouse is nothing short of amazing. With the floor-to-ceiling windows, sleek hardwood floors, and modern furniture, everything about the place screams single male and excess wealth.

"Make yourself comfortable," he says as he tosses his keys on a table near the door.

I walk toward the windows, soaking in the decadence. The city lights twinkle in the distance like a cloudless sky, sparkling against an endless backdrop. "The city's beautiful from up here."

Leo stands behind me, his body heat licking at my

back. "I've spent many nights staring out across the city."

I smile over my shoulder, but I don't let my gaze linger too long. His cocky smile and luscious mouth are like my kryptonite, making it almost impossible for me to hold true to my promise to be done with him. "I can see why. It's so beautiful," I say, keeping my focus on the skyline in front of me.

"Want to sit outside?"

"Yes," I say quickly. I know staying inside means we'd sit on the couch, and the likelihood I'd end up in Leo's lap or in his bed is extremely high. I need to maintain a safe distance because my willpower around him is damn near nonexistent.

Leo grabs a bottle of red and two wineglasses before I follow him onto the patio. I'm not planning on staying long enough to polish off a bottle, but Leo doesn't seem to care. I settle into the chair near the railing, on the opposite side of the table, and swallow down my fear of heights.

The best course of action is to get right to the point and not to veer off topic. "What did you want to talk about?"

Leo stares at me for a moment as he pours two glasses. I drink him in, noticing the silver cuff links sparkling like the stars above our head. They're expensive, just like his penthouse.

"I need to know who saw us at the airport."

"You're not going to..." I pause and look out across

the city, wondering if I should tell Leo the man's name. While the physical attraction to Leo is undeniable, I don't know enough about him to know if he's dangerous or not. I bring my gaze to his and soak in his piercing eyes. "You know..."

"I'm not going to hurt anyone, Daphne. I'm not my father," he says.

"Fine. All I know is his name is Billy. I don't know a last name or what he does, but he knows my brother and was all too quick to call him and report on my whereabouts."

"I'll take care of him." He hands me a wineglass like he didn't just say he was going to off someone, and my eyes widen in horror. "I'll talk to him," Leo corrects and shakes his head slowly. "Again, I'm as much like my father as you are yours. Stop thinking the worst of me."

I glance down, running my fingers along the base of the wineglass. I feel so out of place and like a fool. "What are we doing here, Leo?"

"Talking," he says like it's that simple.

"I know that, but why?" My gaze flickers to his for a brief second, but the lust is too strong, and I have to look away. "I told you we were through. I sound like a broken record at this point."

"If my father wasn't my father and your father wasn't yours, would you still be telling me there's no future for us?"

I don't answer right away. I ponder the question

along with the complexity and simplicity of the entire situation. I want to lie to him. It would be easier for both of us if this were nothing more than a passing attraction. I really wish I'd fucked him out of my system, but that only seemed to make matters worse.

"I don't know," I say honestly. "You're busy. I'm busy. There's not much time to plan a future when we're both dedicated to our work."

He studies my face, and I can feel the heat of his gaze. "What's more important to you, work or family?"

"Family, of course."

That's a no-brainer. Family always trumps business. It's the main reason we shut down the bar for half the day every Sunday. We decided that we didn't want any interruptions during our family dinner, and there always seemed to be a crisis at the bar that needed our attention.

Leo leans back and undoes the top button on his dress shirt, exposing just enough skin to draw my attention back to him. "Do you want a family of your own someday?"

"Someday," I say in a deeper tone, unable to hide what the sight of him does to me. "But not yet."

His fingers work at more buttons on his shirt. "So, if we were just Leo and Daphne, not Conti and Gallo, we'd have a shot?"

He knows what he's doing to me. The smirk on his face tells me as much. It's only fair since I toyed with him near the elevators first.

"Maybe," I sigh and look away. "Who knows. I don't spend much time thinking about what could be when reality seems to smack me in the face every day, constantly reminding me I'm a Gallo."

"My father questioned me today," he confesses.

"About us?" I swallow the lump that's now lodged in my throat.

"No, but he heard I was in the old neighborhood." Leo rubs his hand across his face, trying to cover the frown I know is there. "He warned me to stay away. He said your father was a dangerous man."

I laugh at the stupidity of the entire situation. "See? We would never work."

"Maybe," he admits as his gaze drops to his wineglass. "But I've never been one to let my father dictate my life."

"Me either." But that doesn't mean I don't heed my father's warning every once in a while.

Leo leans forward and pushes his glass to the side. "I'm not ready to give up on whatever this is, Daphne." He slides his hand across the tabletop and places his palm on my arm, reminding me of the sparks I feel every time we touch. "Life's too short to deprive ourselves of finding out."

I stare across the table, wanting to say yes, but something stops me. I could easily fall in love with Leo —hell, I was in full-blown lust already. "I need time to think," I say, hoping it's enough to satisfy him.

"Stay the night."

"I can't." My heart wants to stay, but I know nothing good will come from another night with Leo. I'll fall a little harder and a little deeper, making my ability to resist him even weaker.

"Another time, then."

I shake my head, because there won't be another time. There can't be. "You're persistent."

His stare intensifies. "Only when I know what I want."

I pretend to ignore his statement even though my stomach flutters and my heart practically skips a beat. "I think I should go." I need to get away from him before we fall into bed and I never want to go back to reality.

"I'll take you back to the bar."

"No," I say quickly. "I'll grab a cab."

"It's late, and the bar is far, Daphne. Don't be silly."

My phone rings in my purse, and I scramble to answer it, without looking at the caller ID. It's well after midnight, and there's never good news at this hour. "Hello," I say, watching Leo across the table.

"Where the fuck are you?" Michelle asks. "Your Jeep is here, but you're not. Angelo is going to stroke out when he notices."

"Tell him I'll be back in thirty minutes. I had to help a friend or something."

"Are you with him?"

"Michelle..."

"Daphne, so help me God—" she starts to say, ready to give me a lecture, but I cut her off.

"Don't breathe a word to my brother. Cover for me."

"I'm not a good liar," she tells me like I don't already know this. "I'll buy you some time, but you better get your ass back here because I can only entertain him for so long."

"Find a way," I say. "Flirt with him or something."

There's a pause from the other end. "I'll do my best."

I jam my phone back into my purse as I stand. "I have to leave now. Things are getting too complicated, and someone's bound to find out."

Leo follows me to the door. "This is it, then?" he asks, and the look in his eyes tugs at my heart.

"We're both in danger. This has to be the end." My voice wavers on the last few words.

Leo moves closer. "I want things to be different."

I resist the urge to say the same thing. It won't make this easier or change anything. We can wish all we want, but that won't do a damn thing. I'll still be a Gallo, and he'll be a Conti, making any type of relationship between us impossible.

He snakes his arm around my back and pulls my body flush against his. He's staring into my eyes, intense as always, and he leans forward. I love being in his arms, surrounded by his scent and caught in his

121

intense gaze. I slide my hands up his arms, gripping his delicious biceps and tethering myself to him.

"Goodbye, Daphne," he says softly with his lips only a few centimeters away from mine.

My gaze dips to his mouth, hoping he'll kiss me. "Goodbye, Leo," I whisper before locking eyes with him again.

His eyes search mine, and all the air inside his penthouse evaporates. My breathing's shallow as I wait for the moment his lips touch mine, praying he'll kiss me one last time. The wait isn't long before he leans forward, bringing me closer, and crashes his mouth down on top of mine.

Any breath I have left is instantly stolen. His kiss is demanding, rough, and makes my toes curl. There's no goodbye in the way his tongue slides against mine. Only a promise of something more, something better.

I pull away, breaking the kiss before I become too consumed and lose the willpower to walk out the door. My grip on his arms increases as I hold him at a distance and gasp for air.

He stares at me, breathing just as heavily as I am, but he doesn't say a word. I can't bring myself to say goodbye again, but I know I have to leave. Without speaking, I back up, waiting until the last moment to pull my hands away from his body and open the door. Leo stands in the hall, watching as I walk backward into the hallway, eyes locked on his for only a few seconds before turning my back and heading toward the elevator.

Why is it so damn hard to say goodbye to him? I don't love the man, but the lust is there and totally undeniable.

A week ago, I barely knew the name Leo Conti, but now... Now, I can't seem to get him out of my system.

CHAPTER ELEVEN

DAPHNE

ONE MONTH later

"DAPHNE!" Vinnie yells from the other room as he slams the front door, making me jump. "I'm home."

It's been four weeks since Vinnie went back to college and I said goodbye to Leo. They've also been the longest thirty days of my entire life. Every few days, Leo has two dozen red roses delivered to my place with nothing but the letter L on the card. They're constant reminders of what could've been if

I'd only said yes, but I know I made the right decision, even if my heart doesn't agree.

I drop the pillow I've been holding and run into the living room. "Vinnie!" Flinging my arms around him, I pepper his face with kisses, happy he's here and hoping he'll get my mind off Leo for a few days.

"Hey!" Vinnie wraps his massive arms around me, lifts me off the floor, and spins us in a circle. "I knew you missed me."

"You're an asshole." I laugh.

His head jerks back, and he looks hurt. "What did I do now?"

"It's been a month since you've been home. We've all missed you." I squeeze him one more time before finding my footing.

He laughs and shakes his head, showing off his cute dimples. "You know where to find me, sis."

Even though he's in his junior year, I still haven't gotten used to Vinnie being gone so much. During football season, he barely made it home because of the grueling travel schedule and never-ending workouts and practices.

"You look bigger." I take a step back and stare at him. "Soon you're going to be so big you're going to look like one of those guys with a shrunken head from *Beetlejuice.*"

He's almost as tall as Angelo and Lucio, with the same thick mocha eyebrows, but his hair matches mine, filled with warm caramel browns and streaks of chocolate. His arms have grown, becoming thicker and more defined, looking more like a man than a kid these days.

"Beetle-what?"

"Never mind." I shake my head, wishing the kid would expand his horizons and taste in movies just a little bit beyond *The Fast and the Furious*.

"Shut up," he teases and shows off his way-too-big muscles, flexing them repeatedly. "I've been bulking for football."

"Uh, yeah. I can see that." I wave my hands in his direction and mock him by hunching my shoulders and raising them near my head like the Hulk. "How do I look?" I say in a deep, macho voice, stalking around my apartment like an idiot.

The perfect V in the center of his top lip flattens as he crosses his arms in front of his chest and glares at me with his striking green eyes. "Like an idiot."

"It's like lookin' in the mirror, huh?" I giggle as I continue to act a fool, and Vinnie can't help but laugh too.

"Are you going to be a pain in my ass all weekend?"

"I'm sure you're the *big* man on campus. Someone has to give you a reality check, little brother." I head toward the bedroom I made up for him. "Come on. Get settled. I've got to go to work."

He leans against the doorframe, studying me as I finish making up the guest bed for him. "You look thinner," he says softly as he studies me.

"Is that how you compliment all the ladies?

Because you're going to be single forever with lines like that." I punch the pillow and toss it near the headboard.

"No. You look good, sis. I'm just wondering why you look thinner."

I place my hands on my hips and glare at him. "I started working out. Why?"

He raises his hands in the air when I start to move toward him. "Just making an observation. As long as you're doing it the right way and not starving yourself to become a bean pole like you did after the Tommy Pasquale incident."

I blow a piece of hair away from my eyes that had fallen during my tug-of-war with the sheets that never seem to want to fit over the mattress.

"Unpack and settle in," I tell him before brushing past him in the doorway. I don't feel like rehashing the past with my little brother or explaining how my heart was a little broken after saying goodbye to Leo. "I've got to get to work."

"Okay." He stalks into the living room and stretches, barely able to hold back a yawn. "I'm going to come help out at the bar tonight."

My eyebrows shoot up because Vinnie never wants to work. "You are?"

"I figure you could use some help."

My mouth hangs open, and I blink at him, wondering if I heard him right. "Say that again."

"I figure you could use some help."

The only reason Vinnie would want to work is pussy. It's his driving force in life. Well, women and football, to be exact. "If you're planning on hooking up with some barfly, don't even think about bringing them back here. If you come there to work, that's fine, but it's not a pussy buffet."

"Come on, sis," he pleads with an innocent face. His dimples deepen, making him look sweet, when he's the furthest thing from it.

Vinnie has always caused trouble, but usually, Angelo and Lucio would get blamed because people thought Vinnie was an angel. The boy had trouble-maker written all over his face, but it seemed to be visible only to us and nobody else.

"Keep that shit in your pants." I point toward his lower half. "We don't need some neighborhood skank trying to get knocked up by the great Vinnie Gallo. You got me?"

"If I pick someone up, I promise I'll put a raincoat on it."

I gag, being overdramatic, but he's still my little brother. The thought of anyone wanting to have sex with him is just plain gross. "Just cover that shit. I'd hate for you to drop out of college because of a quick fuck."

"Quick?" A smirk dances on his lips. "I'm never quick."

"Shut up." I punch his shoulder playfully.

"How's Ma?"

"Nuttier than ever. You'll see."

"I've missed her," he admits with a soft smile.

"Well, you'll get your fill this weekend."

Vinnie glances around, and I realize I haven't thrown out last week's flowers or the ones before that. They're wilted, and they look awful. "Someone likes you. Anything you want to tell me?"

I roll my eyes. "No. They're from a friend."

"I don't send roses to my friends." He smirks.

"I have to get to the bar," I tell him, changing the subject.

He yawns, walking back to his room and stretching before collapsing back onto the bed. "I'm going to close my eyes for a minute, and I'll be over."

"Sure," I mutter.

Vinnie is notorious for breaking promises—he has that much in common with my father.

"I swear to God, I'll be there. Don't give me shit. It was a long drive." He's so full of it. His college is a whopping two-hour drive from my place. That does not constitute a long drive in anyone's book.

"Bye." I close the door, leaving him to get his beauty sleep.

"DID VINNIE MAKE IT OKAY?" Angelo asks from behind the bar before I even have two feet inside Hook & Hustle.

"Depends on what your idea of okay is."

He looks up for a moment and quirks an eyebrow. "Is he alive, at least?"

"Yeah, yeah. He's alive and napping." I shove my purse under the counter, wishing like hell I was napping too.

Angelo goes back to studying a stack of papers, running his pen down the sheet before flipping to the next page. "Is that what it's like to be in college?"

"What? Laziness? I don't fucking think so."

"Must be a jock thing," Lucio says as he walks into the front of the bar, overhearing our conversation.

"I'm sure he gets an easy ride because he's the star football player," I tell them, remembering the shit he got out of doing in high school. "It's bullshit, but it's always been that way with him."

"It's just a good thing he can actually read and write with all the homework he didn't have to do," Lucio says and starts to laugh. "That little prick."

"Speaking of little pricks." Angelo smirks and turns his attention to Lucio. "How's the wife?" he asks.

I walk away as they start to talk about the honeymoon phase, something I know nothing about. At the rate I'm going, I'm not sure I'll ever experience being that blissfully happy either.

"Tino!" a few old-timers yell as my father walks through the front door, making a spectacle and a grand entrance.

He strolls through the crowd, shaking hands with

his friends like he's a celebrity, before making his way to me. "Hey, doll, how's business tonight?"

He's been back a month now, but the man hasn't put in an hour's work at the bar, even though he's required to as part of his early release program.

I grab a glass, trying not to get an attitude. "Busy as always, Dad. Want to help?"

He takes a step back and clears his throat. "I can't tonight, Daphne. I'm pretty busy."

"Yeah," I mumble. "Sure looks like it."

He runs his hand through his salt-and-pepper hair and motions over his shoulder. "Well, I better go check on your mother."

I nod because it doesn't matter what I say, he's not going to pitch in. There's no use wasting my breath. "She's out back."

"Don't worry. He's still adjusting," Michelle tells me as she shoves a tip into her front pocket.

"Did your dad act like this when he got out?"

"He wasn't himself for a while, but he slowly got back into the groove," she says while she checks her makeup in the mirror behind the bar.

My dad didn't have a groove.

He had a way of life.

Even though he was released early for time served and good behavior, I have a nagging feeling he's fallen back into the lifestyle—the very one that landed him in the joint in the first place.

I settle into my usual routine, checking on the

customers, chitchatting with the regulars about life, sports, and all the juicy neighborhood gossip. Hours pass and Vinnie's still MIA, but the bar is slammed and selling out of liquor at twice the rate as usual.

Michelle follows me into the back room and collapses onto a crate of vodka. "You look like shit," she tells me point-blank as I pull down a bottle of tequila from the top shelf.

"Thanks." I give her a fake smile, knowing I feel like shit too.

"Let's go out tomorrow. You need some fun in your life. You've been sulking for a month, and I can't take much more."

"I have plenty of fun in my life, and for your information, I have not been sulking."

"Sure." She cackles. "You're a party animal," she says, picking at her fingernails and twisting her lips.

"I have plenty of fun," I repeat, feeling defensive. "We have to work."

"Working doesn't mean fun. Come out with me, and I'll show you what fun really means." She challenges me because she knows I won't back down. "Vinnie can fill in."

I walked right into that one, but Vinnie will be my saving grace. "Fine. I'm game." My stomach churns even thinking about the killer hangover I'll have from this night of *fun* she's talking about.

She rubs her hands together and smiles. "I know

just what we're doing too. We're going to find you a piece of ass so you forget all about Leo."

I blanch, not looking for a random hookup. "I don't need ass, and I forgot about him a long time ago."

She purses her lips. "You definitely need a guy, and you're not fooling anyone. You've been sour since the day you ended things with him."

I wave my hands in the air, showing my surrender, and walk into the hallway, leaving her behind. I'm not even five feet away when Michelle's hand lands on the fleshy part of my ass.

I yelp and glare at her over my shoulder.

"Yeah, you need some bad." She laughs.

"Vinnie!" Angelo yells across the bar when boy wonder walks in just as I walk out of the hallway from the back room.

Vinnie waves, looking so much like my father it's scary. He doesn't shake hands like Santino, but he sure has the look of importance down like he's waving to his adoring fans.

People in the bar start to murmur about the kid who went to Ignatius Prep and helped bring home a state championship in football for the neighborhood. Now every Saturday during college football season, the only thing on at the bar is Vinnie's football game. We have a viewing party and cheer him on as he runs downfield, carrying the ball toward the end zone like the cops are chasing his ass.

My mom runs right to Vinnie. "Oh, my baby." She

holds his face in her hands before she starts to pepper him with kisses much the same way I did. "You look so good." She's gushing over him.

Vinnie turns beet red, but he stays still and lets her embarrass him. "I've missed you, Ma."

"Let me look at you," she tells him and backs up a bit, leaving her hands cupping his cheeks. "You're looking good, kid."

"I've been working out." And right on cue, he flexes like the meathead he always has been and probably always will be.

She tries to wrap her hands around his biceps for a second, sticking her tongue out like she's doing something impossible. "I can tell. I can't even touch my fingertips around these guns."

"Ma, you haven't been able to do that since I was twelve."

"Finally. Ready to work?" I ask him, saving him before she does something else to embarrass him.

He glances at me out of the corner of his eye. "If I must," he says, always being whiny when it comes to anything that resembles manual labor.

"The last time I checked, you are still part owner of this place too."

"I'm the hook," he says with his chin raised and filled with cockiness. "The rest of you are the hustle."

"Whatever." I grab a towel off the counter before tossing it at him.

It smacks him in the side of the face. "Thanks," he

mumbles behind the rag before peeling it away. "I'm more of a bartender, though."

"Wash the tables," I tell him and motion around the bar. "There's a lot of dirt to clean up around here."

He walks up to me and drops his voice, "Where are all the hot women?"

"Slumming it elsewhere."

"Fuck," he hisses. "I was hoping to have a little fun this weekend."

"Oh, I'm sure some trashy bimbo will walk in here at some point. Word's already spreading that you're here."

He pulls his phone from his pocket and makes flirty faces into the screen, practicing. "Maybe this will bring the girls to the yard."

My brother's ego has grown almost as big as his large Gallo head. "Don't worry, pretty boy. You look perfect. Not even a hair out of place."

He ignores me and talks into the camera. "Hey, ladies. I'm back in town and down at my bar, Hook & Hustle. Come on over and see me tonight. If you're lucky, I may even do some push-ups." He winks before pressing a few buttons.

"You're unbelievable," I mutter.

"That's what she said." He laughs.

I just shake my head and walk away.

CHAPTER TWELVE

DAPHNE

I'm barely awake, and it's already noon. I haven't even had an entire cup of coffee when Vinnie strolls through the front door with the biggest smile on his face. He strides into the kitchen, wearing the same clothes he had on last night, only with a few more wrinkles. He slides onto the stool across the counter from me and taps his hands against the granite. "How's your morning going?"

"I haven't decided yet. It's too early to think," I grumble into my coffee mug.

I've never been much of a morning person, and that's probably why working at the bar suits me so well. I can sleep in whenever I want and never have to worry about setting an alarm. My brother is obviously a morning person, or he wouldn't be so damn chipper at this hour.

He stares down at his reflection in the polished black granite. "Mine's going amazing." He peeks up at me for a few seconds before going back to admiring himself. "Thanks for asking."

"Fucker," I whisper.

"What?"

"Nothing."

"So, Michelle and I were talking last night."

The cup is halfway to my mouth when I stop. "Please tell me you didn't sleep with her."

"She said she wants to take you out. That you need a break from working, and since I'm in town..." he continues without providing me any reassurance he didn't try to get into Michelle's pants. He stares straight into my eyes and says something I never expected. "I'm going to cover your shift so you two can have a night out."

I put my cup down and try to comprehend how any of this makes sense. Vinnie is never the first one to volunteer for anything. "Vinnie, I love you, but..." My voice trails off.

But then I think about it. The bar is partially his,

and he needs to put in some time like the rest of us. He's collecting checks every month from the profits; he may as well earn a little of the money too.

"I think you're right. It's a great idea."

"Is it?" His mouth hangs open.

"It is."

I don't really care about going out with Michelle, but I think he deserves to walk a mile in our shoes.

"Well, okay then," he says quickly.

"Are you sure?" I ask, giving him one more out and expecting him to take it.

"Completely. Last night was a breeze. I'm sure tonight will be more of the same."

I don't bother telling him Saturday night is always more crowded than Friday. Last night, we were slammed after people heard he was back in town. Tonight, it will be worse. But Vinnie seemed to handle everything in stride.

All the little neighborhood women, both young and old, would be there to get a glimpse of Vinnie Gallo— the Italian football god with pristine olive skin and green eyes.

"You're smart. I'm sure you can handle it," I reassure him, even though I'm not entirely convinced.

He covers his mouth to stifle a yawn. "I'm going to lie down for a bit. Those girls exhausted me last night."

"Girls?"

"Three," he says with a smug grin.

There's no point in lecturing him about sleeping with customers. Vinnie's going to do whatever he wants, when he wants, how he wants. We've all given him the sex talk. The rest is up to him. "Go rest. You're going to need it tonight."

"Oh, I know." His dimples appear as he rubs his hands together. "I'm hoping for round two."

My eyes widen. I shouldn't be surprised by anything or anyone my brother does anymore. "Two nights in a row with the same chicks?"

"Hell no. Variety is the spice of life."

"I'm glad to see you have your priorities in order," I say to him as he walks toward his bedroom.

He turns around, holding the side of the door with his hand. "Wear something nice tonight, and put on some makeup. Michelle has big plans for you."

Before I can reply, he shuts the door, and I can hear his laughter on the other side.

"Fuckers," I mumble. "Both of them."

Those two cooked up something without clueing me in on their little scheme. I send a text to Michelle to get the scoop, and my phone rings as soon as she reads the text message.

"Hello."

"Oh my God, Daphne. I have the best night planned for us."

"Yeah?" I try to sound excited.

"Yes!"

I stare in the mirror, running my finger along the bags under my eyes as she chatters on about how amazing everything is going to be.

"What time are we going out?"

"I'll be there to pick you up at nine, and wear something pretty like a dress or that cute-as-fuck black miniskirt you have tucked away somewhere in the bowels of your closet."

"I have sexy clothes."

"Not since you called it quits with Leo. Anyway, a flannel and jeans do not equal sexy unless you're a lumberjack. Last time I checked, you didn't fit the bill. You've been in a rut, my friend."

I glance down and tug at the edge of my favorite red flannel. "I think I'm pretty hot. And you wore a flannel last night."

"Just look good tonight, or I'm picking out your clothes when I get there."

"Fine," I groan.

"Hey, Daphne," she says before I can hang up.

"Yeah?"

"Shave your bits too." She ends the call before I can ask why it matters. I'm not going to sleep with anyone.

MICHELLE GASPS when I open the front door.

Somehow, I managed to get my favorite pencil skirt on without falling over, and it's hugging all my curves in just the right spots. I feel a little bit like the old Daphne again. The one who didn't spend a month sulking, trying to pretend Leo Conti didn't exist.

"Dayumn!" Her eyes travel down my body, ending at my feet, which are covered in the cutest black high heels.

"I did good?" I touch my cleavage, regretting the new push-up bra I bought last week because my tits look off-the-chain huge.

"You're you again." She whistles, looking impressed. "Someone's going to get lucky."

"I'm not sleeping with anyone tonight, Michelle," I tell her again because she doesn't seem to believe me.

"Did you shave?" She grabs my arm, lifting it high in the air, but I pull it back quickly. "Phew. But did you shave everything?"

"Why do I have to shave everything if I'm not sleeping with anyone?"

"Because you need dick badly, and no man wants a bush."

I roll my eyes and already know this is going to be a very long night.

THIRTY MINUTES LATER, we're standing outside,

waiting in line for a nightclub on the North Side. "What is this place?"

"It's the hottest club right now." She reapplies her lip gloss for the tenth time since we stepped out of the car.

"This doesn't look like much of a club." I peer up at the building, and it looks like it should've been condemned ten years ago.

"Look at the line." She motions to the people behind us with the tube still in her hand. "There's the proof. Looks can be deceiving. Kind of like you in that flannel. You look frumpy, but you clean up nice."

"Watch it. I always look good. I just don't need to get all dolled up every day for Johnny and the guys at the bar."

"You never know who's walking through that door, princess. You're not getting any younger either. Stop dwelling on a guy you can't have and look for one you can ride—" she pauses and giggles "—into the sunset with."

"Michelle, baby. I've missed you," the bouncer says and totally catches me off guard. I've never been here, but Michelle's obviously been here enough to make friends with the guy.

"Hey, handsome," Michelle says flirtatiously before kissing him on the cheek. "I haven't seen you in a while."

"No man tonight?" he asks.

Man? I can't remember the last time Michelle had

a boyfriend, but it's been at least a year. This club hasn't even been open that long.

"Just my girl." She knocks her shoulder into me.

"You're holding up the line here!" someone behind us yells.

The bouncer glares down the sidewalk, and his black eyes narrow on the crowd. "The natives are getting restless. You ladies be careful in there. If you need anything, let me know."

She nods and pulls me inside the doors before people start throwing shit at the backs of our heads. "Man, they're vicious out there," she says as we step into the dark corridor with a faint light at the other end.

"How come I've never met your friend, and who's the guy you come here with?" I ask as the walls rattle around us from the thumping bass.

"Walk faster." She tugs on my arm and ignores my question. "We're missing the action."

When we reach the light, I'm momentarily blinded. I cover my eyes with my hands, and I blink a few times, trying to let my vision adjust. I spread my fingers apart slowly and take in the sight before me. "Holy fuck!"

"Come on," she mouths, her voice drowned out by the wicked beat.

As we walk, I bump into no fewer than twenty people, but no one seems to mind. People are dancing, intoxicated by the music, booze, and probably drugs too. They're too wasted to even care that I almost knock them over.

Once we're at the bar, Michelle holds up two fingers to the bartender like she's a regular.

"You like?" she yells in my ear, jutting her chin out toward the dance floor.

I shrug. I haven't decided what I think yet. I can't wrap my mind around this place. From the outside, it looks like a run-down building, though the inside is anything but.

There're massive columns with cages on top scattered throughout the large room with barely dressed women writhing inside. The DJ booth at the other end is lit up in red with a small crowd inside, jumping up and down to the beat. There have to be easily a thousand people in here.

Michelle bumps my arm and holds out a martini glass filled with something purple. I don't bother to ask what it is because I can't hear shit anyway. She pushes it toward my lips. "Drink it," she says, or at least, that's what I think she says because I still can't hear her.

Blackberry dances across my tongue as I take my first mouthful. My insides are rattling with each thump and beat as one song bleeds into another while I sip my martini.

Michelle motions toward the dance floor with her thumb and tells me to drink up. In the too-high but super-cute heels, I stagger toward the dance floor and toss back the last drop of the martini. I set the empty glass on a table before I step onto the shiny black tile with a crowd so large I can't even see the other side.

I've never claimed to be an amazing dancer, but with the intoxicating beat and the dim lighting, I feel sexy again. My body's moving, flowing with the rhythm as I dance around Michelle. She's busting moves that I haven't seen her make since high school prom.

My body's flushed and covered in sweat, but I push my embarrassment aside and keep on dancing with Michelle. She's eating it up, dropping to the floor like something straight out of a music video.

When the song ends and the group around us claps, we bow together and break out into laughter as we run off the dance floor like we're kids again. We wind our way down another hallway, different from the one we entered through, until it opens onto a giant courtyard.

"Let's get another drink and cool off out here."

The patio is lined with the tropical trees and over-head twinkling white lights against the starry sky.

I jostle from foot-to-foot, eyeing the only empty table across the patio. "I need to sit." I don't even need to look to know a blister is starting to form and the skin near my Achilles tendon is wearing away.

"Find a seat, and I'll get the drinks," she tells me before walking away.

I stand there for a moment, watching Michelle as she heads toward the bar, before I take a step. I don't even make it more than a few feet before I collide with something solid, someone big.

I stumble backward, ready to fall until strong hands wrap around my arms. "Sorry," I say, lifting my face to see the one man I came here to forget.

Fuck.

CHAPTER THIRTEEN

LEO

"Leo," she says with wide eyes. "What are you doing here?"

"I know the owner and stopped in for a quick meeting," I lie because I don't want her to know I tracked her down.

I do actually know the owner, but my visit to the club has nothing to do with business and everything to do with Daphne.

I took a big risk. I went to Hook & Hustle, hoping no one would recognize me, and paid a waitress a hundred bucks to tell me where Daphne was. I went there with every intention of talking to her, but when I found out she took the night off, I knew this was my chance.

"Oh. Well." She glances down at her feet. "I don't want to keep you."

"How have you been?" I ask, trying to find a way to keep the conversation going and feeling her out.

"Really well." She gives me a fake smile. "And you?"

"Good." There's an awkward pause as we stare at each other.

She's so beautiful. The month apart was harder than I expected. I sent flowers every few days, making sure she didn't forget about me and always knew I was thinking about her. "Can I buy you a drink?"

Daphne glances over her shoulder, and my eyes follow hers to Michelle. "It's probably best if you don't."

I reach over and brush her hair off her shoulder, touching her skin with the backs of my fingers. Daphne doesn't pull away, and I know she's struggling as much as I am. "Just one," I beg.

Daphne turns again, looking toward her friend. "Michelle doesn't like you much."

"Well then, it's a good thing I'm not interested in Michelle. Please sit," I tell her, pulling out a chair at the table next to us. "I'll be right back."

"Don't be too long," she says as she sits down and relaxes back into the chair.

As soon as I order our drinks, Michelle walks over, tapping her fingernail against her glass. "I don't like you," she tells me, reinforcing what Daphne has already told me.

"I know."

"You're dangerous."

"I'm not." I keep my cool, knowing if I don't win over the best friend, there's no hope of ever getting Daphne. "My father may be—just like Daphne's—but I am not dangerous."

Michelle eyes me. "What are your intentions toward my best friend?" She raises an eyebrow and cocks her head.

"Intentions?"

She nods. "Are you just playing with her heart, or are you more into the whole mindfuck thing?"

"Neither." I turn toward Michelle and rest my elbow on the bar. "Have you ever met someone and wanted them so badly you can't even explain it?"

"Well, maybe," she says and fidgets with the drink in her hand as she glances down at the floor.

The only thing I can do is lay all my cards on the table. "Listen, I know there're a million reasons why we shouldn't be together, but none of them matters because of how I feel about her."

Michelle drops her chin and peers up at me. "And that would be?"

I've never been one to talk openly about my feelings, especially with a stranger. But I know Michelle's

151

the key to my ever having a chance with Daphne, and that means I have to be open and honest.

"I love her." The words slide off my tongue with ease. Maybe because I'm not saying them to Daphne's face, but professing them to her best friend. "I know it's crazy. We barely know each other, but..."

"No," she says, cutting me off. "It's not crazy." Her words shock me. "I've known Daphne my entire life, and I've never seen her so tied up in knots over someone." She leans forward and drops her voice. "She'd kill me for saying this, but I think she loves you too. I've never seen her as miserable as I have the last month."

"Then I have to set shit straight and get my girl," I tell Michelle.

"Daphne isn't the obstacle. It's your father and hers that are the issue. I've warned Daphne about you, told her to stay away. But I can't do it anymore. I've never seen her so sad, and I can tell you care for her. I'll give my blessing and bow out tonight, giving you two time together."

"You'd do that?" I'm shocked Michelle is so willing to give us tonight.

"Of course." She smiles and glances in Daphne's direction. "Just figure out a way to make shit right, or you won't have to worry about Santino Gallo. I'll hunt you down myself."

I laugh. Michelle's small, but I can see the same fierceness in her eyes I see in Daphne's. "I'll figure out a way."

I've made multimillion-dollar business deals before. Our fathers are no different. They're driven by the dollar and ego. I just have to tap in to how the relationship could benefit them in order for them to call a truce, making an opening for Daphne and me to be together. It sounds simple enough, but I know their egos will be the problem. If Santino is anything like my father, I'm going to have an uphill battle.

"I know what it's like when you want to be with someone so badly your chest hurts," she admits. "I'll never give up hope, and I don't think Daphne's ready to walk away from you either. Now, go," she tells me and shoos me away from the bar. "Make me believe true love is possible against all the odds."

Concern's written all over Daphne's face as I walk toward the table with our drinks in hand, ready to spill my guts. This is new territory for me. I've never wanted someone like I want Daphne, and sharing my feelings isn't something I'm used to either.

"Where's Michelle going?" she asks as I sit down and place a whiskey neat in front of her.

I glance over my shoulder, seeing Michelle head back into the nightclub. "She's giving us time alone."

"Why?" Daphne's eyes widen. "That's not like Michelle."

I don't want to go into detail, telling Daphne how I basically poured my heart out to Michelle and professed my feelings to her best friend. The first time I say the words, I want them to be special...to mean something. I don't want to say them in a trendy nightclub where the seriousness of them will have less impact.

I take her hand in mine. "I can be very convincing." I smirk.

"I'm sure you can," she whispers when I swipe my thumb across the back of her hand.

The sparks are there. Flying all around us in the thick night air. I feel it. She feels it. There's no denying the connection we have. No matter what's between our fathers, it has nothing to do with us—two people with no interest in their businesses—falling for each other.

"I've missed you," I confess, and the words come out easier than I expect.

"I..."

I hang on her words, waiting to hear she feels exactly the same.

She gives me a small smile, blinking slowly across the table from me. "This is crazy, Leo."

There's no sanity in what's happening between us. "Did you miss me?" I ask her point-blank. "Nothing else matters."

"I did," she says and sighs. "I shouldn't have, damn it, but I did, which is insane."

"Then we're both crazy." I laugh and squeeze her hand. "I'll make things right."

Her fingers curl around mine. "How?"

That's the million-dollar question. There're two stubborn, old-fashioned Italian men standing in my way. I have to convince them that we're stronger together than apart. There's nothing easy about it, but I have to face the two men who're driving an invisible wedge between us.

"Don't worry about it. Let me handle things. I'd move mountains to be with you, Daphne."

"Do you understand how irrational this all is? We've known each other what...a month? I shouldn't feel the way I feel about you."

I can't hide my smile. "Sometimes the best things in life go against reason."

"Take me home," she says, and no other words need to be spoken.

The drive back to my place feels ridiculously long. Daphne hasn't stopped stroking my arm from the moment we pulled away from the valet. The second I get her alone in the elevator, I'm all over her.

Our mouths fuse together as our hands roam across each other's bodies, wanting and needing more.

"God, I want you so bad," I murmur against her lips and grip the back of her neck, holding her tightly.

"I need you," she says as her fingers slide under my dress shirt and splay across my stomach.

We tumble out of the elevator as soon as the doors open. She's in my arms, legs wrapped around my waist, kissing me with so much force my lips burn.

I carry her toward my bedroom, one hand in her hair and the other cupping her ass as she grinds her sweet spot against my impossibly hard cock. I lay her on the bed and cover her body with mine, trying to take this as slow as humanly possible.

I don't want to rush. The plane was pent-up lust, but this is something entirely different. Her hands are sliding through my hair, tugging on the ends as she deepens the kiss and locks her ankles behind my ass.

My lips glide across her jaw until I reach the soft skin on her neck and the spot I know drives her wild. "Don't you dare leave a mark," she tells me.

I smile against her neck. "Not on your neck," I promise her, but anywhere else on her body is fair game. It's childish, I know, but I want there to be no mistake that Daphne Gallo belongs to me.

CHAPTER FOURTEEN

DAPHNE

I'm about to walk into the bar and head up to my parents' for Sunday dinner when Michelle texts me.

Michelle: How did last night go?

Me: Great, but...

I stop typing and hit send. My head is no less jumbled than it was the day before. Spending the night with Leo was everything I thought it would be. The way he made love to me slow and gentle, I felt the connection between us getting stronger and more intense.

Michelle: Life's short, girl. I kind of like Leo, and I don't say that lightly.

I sigh, knowing those words aren't easy for her to say. Michelle understands the precariously sticky situation being with Leo puts us both in.

Me: I just don't want my life to be shorter because of him.

The danger is real, even if my statement is meant to be funny. I can't deny that, at any moment, we'll be found out and one of our fathers will take matters into his own hands. Leo said he'll handle everything and find a way to make peace. But it would take a miracle to bring our families together.

"Hey, stranger."

I jump when I hear Vinnie's voice. "For fuck's sake, don't do that shit."

"Who you texting?" He tries to look over my shoulder, but I put the phone against my chest.

"Michelle."

"Tell her hey. I missed her last night."

"Don't even think about sleeping with Michelle," I tell him, poking him in the shoulder as he walks by me.

"Hey, Michelle's a little too..."

"She's what?"

The thing I know about my brother is he'll sleep with just about any woman on the planet as long as she's willing. It's not that he doesn't have standards, he just loves the female body so much he seems to want to try them all out.

"She's not my type."

I grab his arm as he starts up the stairway to our parents' place with his duffel bag slung over his shoulder. "You don't have a type. What aren't you telling me?"

"Nothing." He doesn't look me in the eye when he speaks, and I know he's hiding something. "You came home late last night, or early, depending on how you look at it." He changes the subject to the one thing I don't want to talk about.

"We're almost late. You better hustle." I point up the staircase, praying he'll drop the subject because the boy is always hungry. "Ma probably already has the food on the table."

Vinnie glances up the stairs, lifting his face in the air, and inhales. "Sausage," he says with a smile. "My favorite. I'll race you."

He looks like the little kid I loved so much as he dashes up the stairs. When he was younger, everything was a competition, and I mean everything. He always wanted to be the fastest at everything he did. Usually, we let him win because he was faster than the rest of us. By the time he was sixteen, there was no competition anymore, but that didn't stop Vinnie from trying.

Vinnie flings the door open, and it crashes against the wall and almost smacks him in the face as it swings back.

"Jesus," my mother mutters as she carries the casserole of sausage, peppers, and potatoes toward the dining room.

"Sorry, Ma. It just smells so damn good, I couldn't stop myself."

"Well, slow down, Speed Racer."

"Who?" Vinnie asks as he scratches the side of his head and follows my mom and the food into the dining room.

Angelo's already in his favorite spot in the living room, arm flung across the back of the couch, looking relaxed. "Hey." He ticks his chin at me. "Have a good night off?"

I run my fingers along the back of the couch but can't bring myself to look him in the eye. "It was relaxing. How was Vinnie last night?"

"He was Vinnie."

"Busy?"

"Packed."

"Hey. Hey," Lucio says as he carries Lulu into the living room and sits down next to Angelo.

"Where's Dee?" I ask, glancing around the living room, expecting to see her cheerful face.

Lucio pitches his head toward the bedrooms. "In Ma's office, coloring with the kids." He bounces Lulu in his lap, peppering her face and neck with kisses and making her laugh.

Delilah is such a good mom, and she's scoring brownie points in the aunt department. I'm failing miserably at spending time with my niece and nephew, especially after I promised I'd be there for them after they lost their mother.

"I have to go see them," I say before making my way down the narrow hallway. Their tiny voices fill the hall, and I watch through the small crack in the door as the three of them color.

"Do you think Daddy will ever find us another mommy?" Tate, my niece, asks Delilah.

I clutch my chest and plaster my back against the wall, fighting the tears that are threatening to fall. I can't imagine losing my mother now and I'm a full-grown woman, but Tate and Brax have experienced that kind of loss at such a young age.

"Oh, sweetie," Delilah says in a soothing tone. "No one can ever replace your mommy."

"I know." Tate's voice is almost a whisper. "But Daddy's so sad all the time, Auntie Dee."

Tate sounds wise beyond her years. In a way, she's been robbed of a happy childhood and has been forced to grow up a little faster than most kids.

"Mama," Brax says in his deep, little-man voice.

"She's not here," Tate tells him sternly. "She's never coming back."

I gasp and cover my mouth, hoping no one heard me. I'm devastated by her words.

"Come here, big man," Delilah coos as I peer around the corner, watching them again.

Tate is standing at her side, holding three crayons in her hand with the other arm wrapped around Dee's back. Brax has his face buried in Delilah's hair and his thick arms snaked around her neck, hugging her.

Delilah looks down at Tate and smiles. "Tate, your mommy's always with you. She watches over you two every day, every moment."

Tate looks around the room, no doubt trying to find her mommy. "I don't see her."

"That's because she's in your heart, sweetheart."

"My heart?" Tate whispers and glances down, pressing her hands to her chest. "She's inside me?" Her little lips part as her mouth hangs open.

"You'll always carry her with you. And maybe someday your daddy will find someone else. You'd like that, wouldn't you?"

Tate nods with her hand still over her heart.

"But when he does, your mommy will always be with you."

"Always?"

"Always."

I wipe away my tears and plaster on a smile before pushing open the door, trying to lighten the mood. "Where're my monsters?" I call out, stalking into the room like I'm going to tickle them.

"Auntie Nee. Auntie Nee," Tate calls out, running across the room and practically leaping into my arms.

I hug her tightly, running my hand down her back in soft, slow strokes. "Hey, doll. I missed you so much," I whisper in her ear. "I love you."

"Love you too, Auntie Nee."

Delilah stares at me and smiles before taking a deep breath, probably happy for the rescue. The conversation was getting heavy even for a seasoned pro like Delilah.

"Dinner," Ma calls out, saving us from having to dive deeper into the conversation.

"Who's hungry?"

Brax screeches loudly, trying to scramble out of Delilah's arms before she has a chance to stand. She lets him go, and he's out the door before Tate's feet can touch the floor.

"Thank you," Delilah says to me as we follow the kids down the hallway toward the dining room. "I was starting to lose it."

"You did well, Dee. I couldn't have handled that conversation like you did."

"Oh, please. You're a natural," she reassures me, and I know she's just being nice.

While I love my niece and nephew, I'd never call myself overly maternal. I want kids someday, but I'm not sure if I could ever be as good of a mother as mine was to us.

"Sit, sit," my father says and stands as we enter the room. I'm almost surprised he's here on time because lately he's been missing more than he's been present. "The food's getting cold."

Pop's a little more enthusiastic than he usually is, and we're all thinking the same thing as we glance at each other around the table. He's about to drop something big on us. Lately, it hasn't been anything good.

I slide into the chair, making faces at Angelo because I figure he knows what's going on.

"This smells delicious, Ma," Vinnie says as my mother scoops out a giant helping onto his plate.

"I know it's your favorite, baby." Ma hands the casserole across the table, letting the rest of us get our own food instead of babying us like she always does Vinnie.

This dish are everybody's favorite because it's the only thing she can cook that's actually edible. She's been known to mess up the easiest recipes. But this one, she's mastered, and it's perfect every time.

"Can you give me the recipe? I'd like to make it for the guys in my frat."

"It's easy. Just throw sausage, potatoes, and peppers in a pan with a full bottle of wine, red or white, along with some water. Then stick everything in the oven, covered, of course, and let it cook for a few hours until the sausage is tender."

"I don't think even I could mess it up," he says and smiles.

My father pulls out my mother's chair and waits for her to sit before he finally decides to tell us what has him flying high. "So, I know you kids think I'm up to my old ways."

There's a collective grumble from around the table because there's no thinking necessary. My dad has barely been around the last month, heading off to God knows where to do who the fuck even knows with him.

"You know your mother and I are planning our wedding," he says.

"Which is when?" Lucio asks between bites.

"In a few months." Pop smiles at my mom, who's beaming as she gives him her complete attention. "Anyway." He clears his throat. "There's a lot of reasons why your mother and I never got married before."

"We know, Pop," Angelo says, and I can hear the annoyance in his voice.

"No, you don't know, son."

"With marriage comes legalities."

That's a word my father has hated his entire life. Legalities. He's highly allergic to anything that resembles law, and that has always included marriage.

The boys are hanging on my father's every word, but I'm starving, having skipped breakfast to make it here on time after a long and very pleasurable evening with Leo.

"Our money and assets have always been in your mother's name so the government couldn't seize everything if I was arrested."

"When," I correct him, covering my mouth with my hand to hide the hunk of steaming potato that's burning my tongue.

My father sighs. "But there's always been one thing, a big thing, that I've allowed my brother to be in charge of over the years."

I wrinkle my nose in surprise. "Huh," I mumble to myself.

"Now that you kids are old enough, and I'm finally cleaning up my act, I've asked Sal to sign those assets back over to me."

"Why now?" Angelo asks, wondering the same damn thing everyone around the table is.

"I thought of it as an insurance policy for my old age."

"What is it?" Vinnie asks before shoveling half a sausage into his mouth.

My mother covers my father's hand with hers. "Just tell them already."

"We're part owners in a winery," he says quickly.

My head jerks back. "What?"

"I thought that was Uncle Sal's," Angelo says, clearly knowing something about the entire thing.

"It's always been ours too, but I never wanted to put your inheritance in jeopardy."

"I have an inheritance?" Vinnie whispers and places his fork down on his plate.

"You do. I've asked Sal to divide up my stock equally between you kids, along with myself. In total, we own a third of the family winery in Italy, which, when divided five ways, is about six percent each."

"What?" I ask again, still in shock.

Growing up, we were never hurting for money. My parents owned the bar, and my father had his other business dealings, always keeping us fed and clothed with a nice roof over our heads. Never in my life did I think we actually had something more. They never spoke about it, and my Uncle Sal left town when I was too young to remember anything.

"So, are we talking about a little bit of money?" Vinnie rubs his hands together, letting greed get the better of him.

"Probably a couple million dollars each," my father says, like he's talking about the weather.

I feel faint. The room starts to spin, and everything goes dark.

CHAPTER FIFTEEN

DAPHNE

"I'm fine," I say for the third time as my family stands around the gurney I'm currently lying on in the emergency room. "This is ridiculous." I start to sit up because I'm ready to leave, but my mother pushes me back down.

"We're not leaving until we find out what's wrong," she tells me.

"I didn't eat this morning. It's no big deal."

"You've never passed out before, Daphne." Angelo stands near my feet with one hand resting against my leg. "We're not taking any chances."

"Come on," I plead, hoping someone will have some common sense. "Dad dropped a bombshell on us. My body went into shock. It's seriously no big deal."

They're staring at me like I'm a wounded animal, waiting for the moment I kick the bucket. I wonder if this is what it's like to be old or dying, and I know I'll hate every moment of it. I think of Carolyn, Angelo's wife, and the way we sat vigil at her bedside for the last week of her life. I hope we brought her comfort, unlike what my family's doing to me in this very moment.

"Ms. Gallo," the doctor says as he pushes aside the cheap yellow curtain that has concealed us from the chaos of the hallways. "I have some test results back."

"What's wrong, Doctor? Is she okay?" My mother's practically in tears, gripping her chest like she's about to hear news of my impending death.

"Maybe it's best if your family leaves the room so we can discuss the results in private."

That is the worst thing the doctor could say.

"Oh. My. God. You're dying," my mother cries out and almost throws herself on top of me.

I run my fingers over her red hair, trying to soothe her. "I have no secrets from my family. Go ahead, Doc."

"First of all, you're not dying," he says right away.

Well, that's a relief. For a minute, I was wondering if he was going to drop some giant bombshell in my lap, turning my entire life upside down. For weeks, I've been worried about how my relationship with Leo could end up with one of us dying, but I never thought some crazy-ass disease would take me before that could happen.

"Oh, thank God." My mother gasps and lifts her head from my chest. "I don't know what I'd do without you."

"Jesus. Everyone needs to calm down." I pretend like I'm not worried. But to be honest, I was petrified after the doctor came in without a smile. Asking me if I wanted my family to leave meant the news wasn't going to be something I expected.

"We're concerned, Daphne," my father tells me like I'm the one acting crazy.

The entire family is staring at the doctor, waiting to hear what the tests have revealed. "Your blood work came back, and surprise," he says and finally cracks a smile, probably thinking this will be a happy moment. "You're pregnant."

My mouth falls open. "But I just had my period. The test has to be wrong."

"How long ago?"

"I don't know. Maybe five weeks."

"So, you missed a month?" he asks.

"Not really. My periods are never on time." After a year of tracking my periods, I chucked the calendar in the trash. There was something up with my ovaries, and I was never a regular girl with a twenty-eight-day cycle.

"The blood test doesn't lie, Ms. Gallo. You are

indeed pregnant. We'll order an ultrasound to make sure the baby is okay since you passed out."

"I didn't eat this morning," I tell him, still thinking he's yanking my leg.

"You'll need to be more careful about eating every few hours, and start prenatal vitamins right away. Other than that, you're completely healthy."

My world's rocked. I blink a few times with my mouth still hanging open as the doctor walks into the hallway, leaving us behind.

"You were with the baby daddy last night, weren't you?" Vinnie says as he pushes against my leg.

I glare at him.

"She was with Michelle," Angelo says, and I instantly want to punch Vinnie in the gut.

"Nuh-uh. She got in at seven this morning."

They're all staring at me like I'm about to tell them everything, but I've never been one to spill my guts.

"Daphne," my mother says, but she's so excited, she's almost shaking. "My baby's going to have a baby."

"Fuck," I hiss, dropping my head to the bed, and stare up at the ceiling.

This is the worst-case scenario. I'm knocked up. A single mother. Not just that, but I'm pregnant with Leo's kid. It's like the big man upstairs has it out for me. Why can't I catch a break?

"Best You'll Ever Have?" Angelo says, reminding me he knows all about the mystery man. Well, at least enough to know I've been seeing someone on the side but not sharing the details.

"The father better be an honorable man," Lucio says as he clenches his hand into a tight fist. "Or we'll have a problem."

"Everyone, stop." I close my eyes and take a deep breath, wishing I could go back in time and remind myself to use a condom.

Vinnie's laughing. "You always think I'm going to knock some chick up, and look at what you've gone and done."

"Vinnie, don't start with me." I glare at him.

Just as I'm about to lose my shit, Michelle comes running into the room. "Oh my God, are you okay?" she asks as she pushes between my brothers, gasping for air. "Angelo called me and said you were in the emergency room."

"I'm fine," I tell her as my teeth grind together. "Just fucking perfect."

"She's knocked up," Vinnie says, still laughing his ass off at the irony.

Michelle's eyes widen.

"Yep." I nod.

"Oh no," she whispers and covers her mouth, looking every bit the way I feel.

Angelo turns to her, tipping his head to the side as he cracks his neck. "You know him?"

"No," Michelle lies. "I didn't know she was seeing

anyone." She shakes her head, but she's a little over the top with her performance.

My heart's pounding against my chest so hard I can barely breathe. I shake my hands, feeling a panic attack about to strike. "I can't," I say, and my voice cracks on the last word. "I can't be a mother."

"I want to know who the guy is," Angelo says again, never letting shit go. "He better step up and take care of his responsibility."

"I'm no one's responsibility," I tell him, wishing they'd all just leave.

I need time to process this.

The baby.

My baby.

Leo's baby.

Our baby.

Just when I think life couldn't get any crazier, God has a way of reminding me I'm not in control.

"Can I have a minute?" I ask as my nose starts to tickle.

"Sure, baby. We'll be right outside," my ma says before she clears the room when no one moves right away.

"Michelle, can you stay?" I ask, knowing I need someone to be with me, and she's the only one who knows everything that's going on.

"Of course," she says, giving Angelo a glance as he steps out of the room.

"Close the curtain and make sure they're gone," I

tell her because I don't want any chance of my family overhearing anything I'm about to say. The blowback would be catastrophic.

Michelle climbs on the gurney, tucking her leg under her bottom and grabs my hand. "Are you okay?" She laces her fingers with mine and squeezes.

"Michelle, this couldn't be any worse," I whisper.

"Why are you whispering?" she whispers back, mocking me.

I tick my chin toward the hallway, knowing full well my entire family is nosy as fuck. "You know how they are listening."

"We'll figure this out."

"How?" I ask, peering up at her with tears in my eyes.

I don't see a way this finishes with a happy ending. The one damn time I have unprotected sex, I get knocked up. *Un-fucking-believable.*

"You're going to have to tell Leo."

I squeeze my eyes shut, letting the tears spill down my cheeks. "He's going to go ballistic."

I'm not sure how I'll break the news to him. I've spent an entire month trying to pretend he never existed, and the entire time, our baby was growing inside my body. God, what if he thinks I was trying to trap him as some part of an evil plan?

"He may surprise you."

"Well, I'm about to surprise him," I say and start to laugh.

"Ms. Gallo," a woman says near the doorway as she pulls a cart behind her. "Are you ready for your ultrasound?"

Michelle goes to stand, but I pull her back down. "Stay with me."

My mother's right behind the ultrasound technician, smiling from ear to ear as she follows her into the room. "I can't believe we're having a baby," she says like she's going to be the one giving birth. "This is so exciting."

"Yeah. Thrilling," I mumble under my breath as she scans my bracelet.

The ultrasound doesn't take very long, and the technician doesn't say much while she takes pictures of my uterus. I stare at the black-and-white screen, trying to figure out what the hell I'm looking at, but I don't see much of anything.

"Did you see a baby?" I ask as she cleans off her equipment and packs up to leave.

"The doctor will be in shortly to go over the ultrasound with you."

Her words don't give me comfort. "Everything will be fine," my ma says, but she doesn't understand the absolute mess I've created.

Moments later, the doctor walks in, holding the ultrasound pictures in his hand. "Everything looks good, Ms. Gallo. You're around four weeks into your pregnancy. You'll want to follow up with your

OB/GYN this week, but as of right now, both mom and baby are perfectly healthy."

"Great," I say, trying to plaster on a fake smile.

"Here's the first photos." He hands me the sheet of paper and points to a tiny speck. "There's your baby. Congratulations."

"I have to go tell everyone the baby's okay," my ma says before kissing me on the cheek and leaving Michelle and me alone.

I stare at the photo and try to think of the best way to break the news to Leo. For a minute, I think about not telling him. Breaking up with him would probably be the best solution. His life would remain uncomplicated, and our secret would stay hidden.

"Don't even think it," Michelle says as I climb off the gurney and reach for my clothes.

"What?"

"You have to tell him," she says with her arms crossed in front of her chest like she's reading my mind.

"All right. I'll tell him."

"Promise?"

"Promise."

CHAPTER SIXTEEN

LEO

"Mr. Conti, there's a woman on the line for you," my assistant, Katie, says as she stands in the doorway to my office after I hang up with some investors from Australia.

"Who is it?" I rub my eyes after staring at the computer screen for far too long.

"She wouldn't give her name." Katie shrugs. "But she said it's urgent."

"I'll take it." I reach for the phone, seeing the red blinking light for line one. "Please close the door. And,

Katie, you can go home. It's late, and I really appreciate you being here on a Sunday."

"Thank you, Mr. Conti." Katie nods and closes the door behind her, giving me privacy.

"Hello," I say, hoping it's Daphne.

I've been trying to get ahold of her for hours, and she hasn't returned a single text or phone call. I figured she was busy with her family, but with each hour that ticked by, I've become more concerned.

"Leo, we need to talk," she says, and I can tell there's something wrong by the tone of her voice. "But not over the phone."

"Where are you?"

"I'm at home."

"I'll be right there."

"I'll be waiting," she says before disconnecting the call.

I grab my keys, leaving the rest of the work I had left to do sitting on my desk for tomorrow. I rush to her place, driving like a crazy person through the streets of Chicago, not giving two fucks about a ticket or my personal safety. Once there, I slip through the front door of her building as someone walks out instead of using the fire escape.

I knock, trying not to sound too panicked. "Daphne." When she opens the door, I'm struck by the paleness of her skin. "Are you okay?" I take her hand in mine, noticing the hospital bracelet on her wrist.

"What happened?" I ask before she has a chance to answer my previous question.

"I'm fine," she says and pulls me inside. "Close the door before someone sees you."

I kick the door closed, not wanting to take my eyes off her. "Why were you in the hospital? I've been trying to get in touch with you all day."

She walks toward the couch and collapses. "I need you to not freak out."

I rush to her side. "What is it?"

She pulls a pillow into her lap and hugs it tightly. "We have a big problem."

At this point, I'm thinking the worst. Either she's sick or trying to push me away again. I lift her arm and run my thumb underneath the hospital bracelet on her wrist. "Why were you in the hospital?"

"I passed out."

"Why? Did they find something wrong?" I ask, feeling like I've asked her twenty times in the last minute and she hasn't bothered to answer.

"There's no easy way to say this." She pauses and takes a deep breath as her gaze dips to the pillow.

My heart's pounding, and I can barely breathe. Daphne's never been one to beat around the bush, but right now, she can't seem to get the words out. "Just tell me, Daphne."

"I'm pregnant," she blurts out.

My head jerks back. "Say that again?" I'm pretty

sure I heard her wrong because I could swear she said she's pregnant.

She points at me. "You knocked me up."

"Holy shit. You're really pregnant?" My mind is fuzzy, and I'm rocked backward. I'm still not sure I heard her right because my heart's pounding so hard and fast I can barely hear my own thoughts. "You're sure I'm the father?"

I'm not trying to be an asshole. We've slept with each other twice, and the last time was only yesterday. That leaves the plane—where we were so caught up in the moment, we didn't use protection.

She reaches over and hits my chest with the palm of her hand. "It's yours, dammit."

"Mine?" I repeat.

I still can't process the news.

I'm going to be a father.

There will be a little Leo or maybe a tiny Daphne running around the house, squealing with delight.

"Yeah. I'm pregnant with your kid."

The news finally starts to sink in.

"We're having a baby."

"I'm having a baby," she tells me and pulls the pillow tighter against her stomach. "Unless you want to..."

"Don't say it." I hold up my hand, refusing to let her finish the sentence. "I want it." There's no way I'd even think about giving my baby away, or worse, putting an end to the pregnancy. While I'd try to support her if that's what she decided, I want this baby. Our baby.

She sighs. "How's this going to work, Leo? Our families hate each other."

"Our fathers," I correct her. "That has nothing to do with us. They'll have to figure out their own shit." I move closer and pull the pillow away from her. "You're carrying my child." Placing my hand over her stomach, I stare into her brown eyes. "Our baby."

Tears start to stream down her face, and I slide my hands under her legs and pull her into my lap. "I can't believe this is happening." She wipes her tears with the back of her hand as she rests her head against my chest.

"We'll figure it out. We'll get married and raise the baby right."

She sits straight up and blinks a few times. "Married? Are you fucking crazy?"

"Listen," I say, stroking her arms softly, trying to get her to relax. "It makes sense."

"How does anything make sense?" she snaps.

I pull her back against my chest and stroke her hair. "I can't have you and my child living somewhere else, and I most certainly don't want another man to raise my kid as his own."

"Your asshole is showing, Leo."

"Stop, Daphne. I'm being serious. Do you like me, at least?"

She peers up at me. "I've been falling in love with

you, but I'm not ready to talk about marriage. This isn't the 1950s."

I place my fingers under her chin, holding her gaze. "I'm falling for you, Daphne Gallo."

"This is all too soon. Too crazy," she says and bites her lip as she closes her eyes. "I'm not ready for this."

"I don't think anyone's ever really ready, but we will be."

"Leo," she whispers. "We can never get married. We can't even be seen in public together."

I lean forward and press my lips to her forehead. "Let me worry about that, *bella*."

She curls her fingers around my shirt and relaxes in my arms. "I don't have the energy to worry about anything else tonight," she says softly.

"Just rest. I'm not going anywhere," I promise.

Minutes later, she's fast asleep. I kick my feet up, trying to get comfortable. I know I should carry her to bed and leave, but right now, I like having her in my arms way too much to even move.

"Leo," Daphne whispers, brushing her hand softly against my cheek. "Wake up."

"What's wrong?" I grumble with my eyes closed and tighten my arms around her, too comfortable to move.

"You should go. Someone's going to see your car."

I open one eye and glance down at her beautiful face. "I parked down the street. Don't worry. I'm not going anywhere tonight."

"I'm not comfortable."

"With me?"

She shakes her head. "On the couch. I want to sleep in my bed."

"So do I." I slide my arms under her legs and lift her into the air as I stand. I'm not going anywhere tonight unless someone drags me out of here. I'm reeling from the news, and I'm sure Daphne's still in shock too.

I gently place her on the bed and crawl in next to her, curling my body around hers. My hand rests on her stomach, protecting the very spot where our baby's growing.

I ONLY SLEEP a few hours and leave a note on my pillow, telling her I need to get some stuff done and to text me when she's awake. I know I have to find a way to make things right if Daphne and I ever have a chance of being together and keeping our baby safe.

There's only one person who can help. Someone who knows both players and has a vested interest in bringing peace.

I'm sitting outside Hook & Hustle, waiting for any signs of life and trying to figure out what I'm going to say.

The fiery redhead emerges from the front door, looking every bit like Daphne, only smaller. She looks just as I remember her from when I was a little kid, running around this neighborhood.

I slide out of the front seat and stand in between the car and the driver's door, not wanting to get too close and scare the shit out of her.

"Mrs. Gallo," I call out and wave, smiling to put her mind at ease.

Mothers are always the key. Even my hard-ass father always listened to my mother, never wanting to anger her too much.

She stops walking and looks around before her eyes find me. "Yes?"

"I'm Leo."

She eyes me curiously and takes a step closer but still keeps her distance.

"I'd like to talk to you about Daphne."

She tilts her head, and her stare intensifies. "Are you the father?" she asks.

I glance around, knowing being on the street and in front of the Gallo bar probably isn't the safest place for me at the moment. "Can we talk somewhere more private?"

"Answer the question, dear."

I nod. "I am, Mrs. Gallo."

She smiles before glancing up at the building behind her. "Come up for a coffee, and we'll talk."

I shake my head, knowing I can't step foot in the Gallo house. "I can't."

Her eyebrows draw down. "How about the little bakery down the street?"

"I'll give you a ride."

"I'll walk," she tells me, knowing better than to get in a car with a stranger.

Ten minutes later, we're sitting at a table, staring at each other over a fresh cup of coffee and a cannoli. I've spilled my guts, telling her about my relationship with her daughter.

"Leo, give her time. She'll come around," Mrs. Gallo tells me, but I still haven't dropped the biggest problem in her lap.

I move the mug around the table and know I have to come clean. "The problem isn't between Daphne and me, Mrs. Gallo."

"Oh dear." Her eyebrows shoot up. "What is it, then?"

"First, I want to say I'm falling in love with your daughter, and I want to do right by her and our baby."

"Just rip the Band-Aid off and tell me."

"My last name's Conti." I lean back, waiting for her to start yelling or maybe run out of the bakery screaming bloody murder. Worst-case scenario is the little woman is packing heat and decides to end my life right here in the middle of Mazzella's Bakery.

She blinks a few times and stares at me. "Like Mario Conti?" she asks without moving.

"He's my father."

"Oh," she mumbles and touches the base of her

neck, finding the cross hanging from a gold chain. "This is bad."

"I know." I run my palms down and back up my jeans. Bad isn't really the right word for the mess we've created.

"What were you two thinking?" She shakes her head.

"We weren't," I say honestly. "I never expected to fall in love with your daughter, but here I am. In love, with a baby on the way."

Mrs. Gallo leans over the table and wraps her hands around her coffee mug. "So, I take it you're sticking around?"

I nod. "I've asked Daphne to marry me."

Mrs. Gallo glances up toward the ceiling and curses under her breath in Italian. "Did she say yes?"

"She said I was crazy."

She finally cracks a smile, but it quickly vanishes. "Are you part of your father's..."

"No, ma'am. I've never been part of my father's business."

I never would be either. Staying out of the life, his world, was my driving force through college and the reason I worked my ass off to make Excellence the premier hotel chain in the country. I never wanted to be part of his world after seeing the carnage his work caused around the city.

"Well." She pauses, turning her coffee mug in her

hands. "It's not going to be easy, but here's what you need to do."

Mrs. Gallo spends the next hour laying out a plan to help keep Daphne and me both safe. I sit quietly, listening to her talk because she knows both men at the root of the problem. She is wise beyond her years. Daphne's so much like her mother—strong, funny, and beautiful.

"Can you do that?" she asks as soon as she finishes.

"I'll do anything for Daphne and to keep my baby safe," I tell her.

CHAPTER SEVENTEEN

DAPHNE

From two blocks away, I see Leo walking toward the front doors of Hook & Hustle. This can't be good. I scream his name and wave my arms like a maniac, but he doesn't hear me over the police sirens blaring on the next street. Walking faster, I make an effort to focus on my breathing, trying not to have a panic attack at all the ways this could go wrong.

Leo shouldn't be anywhere near the bar. It's too dangerous, between Johnny, my father, and any other men in my father's organization that seem to hang around like barflies. They're always on the lookout and willing to take out any threat before the enemy has a chance to strike first.

I push open the door and gasp.

My father's holding a gun straight out in front of him, and it's pointing at Leo's face. "Get out of here, Daphne," he says, only glancing at me for a moment before bringing his eyes back to Leo.

I don't move. I can't. I'm too petrified that my father will accidentally pull the trigger. "Papa, don't," I plead, clutching my chest as I try to breathe.

"He's the enemy. It's too dangerous for you to be here."

"Mr. Gallo, I'm only here to speak with you," Leo says, but he doesn't move, knowing full well my father wouldn't think twice about killing him.

Angelo walks out of the back room, and his eyes instantly widen. "Pop, what the hell are you doing?"

"Shut up, Angelo," I hiss, wishing he'd go right back into the back room.

"I have nothing to say to a Conti." My father's eyes narrow, and his top lip curls.

"I thought you were leaving the life, Papa," I remind him, still in shock over what I walked in on.

"Take this shit outside," Angelo tells my father, not realizing this isn't shit and the street isn't the place to let the world know I was knocked up by Leo Conti. "You need to leave, Daphne."

I hold my hand up, stopping Angelo as he starts to walk toward me. "Don't," I tell him.

I've never seen this side of my father. Everything he did was hidden away and out of sight. His ruthless side was only spoken about in whispers and during his highly publicized trial.

"I am, baby, but I'll go back to prison to keep you and my family safe."

I can't just stand here and let my dad shoot the father of my baby. "He's the father," I say quickly, not even thinking twice about telling my dad if it means I can save Leo's life.

My father's gaze slices to mine. "He's what?"

"Oh fuck," Angelo mutters and covers his face with his hand.

"Leo and I are in love and we're having this baby, Papa." My hand covers my stomach, instinctively wanting to protect the tiny person inside.

I thought my words would defuse the situation and make my father back down. But so far, it hasn't worked.

"You knocked up my kid?" My father's tone is venomous.

I take a step forward and hold my hand out, motioning for him to give me the gun. "Dad, be reasonable," I say, not scared of my father, but worried for Leo. "We love each other."

"He's a Conti," he repeats like Leo's last name makes one damn bit of a difference to me.

"And I'm a Gallo. Would you want Mario to hold a gun on me?"

"Never," my father answers quickly.

"Please, Mr. Gallo. Let me explain," Leo pleads. "I'm not involved in my father's business. You should know that."

I walk between the gun and Leo, stopping any chance my father will pull the trigger.

"Move," my father tells me, but I remain defiant and still.

"*Bella*," Leo says in that rich, sinful voice that started this entire mess. He grips my arms and lifts me easily off the floor. "Never put yourself in unnecessary danger. The baby." His eyes dip to my stomach as he sets me down at his side. "No one is more important than our baby."

My father's hard, icy glare lessens. "You'd give your life for my kid?"

"The mother of my child," Leo replies, raising his chin without an ounce of fear. "I'd do anything to protect them, even if that means giving my life to keep them safe."

My father finally drops the gun to his side. "How could you two be so stupid?"

This is progress.

"Papa, love isn't always rational." Leo grips my hand tightly as I speak. "We never meant for any of this to happen."

"I'm sorry, Mr. Gallo. I came here to talk to you man-to-man about what happened and ask for your blessing."

"I could've killed you." My father drags his free

hand down his face and groans.

"Put the gun away, Papa." I walk toward him slowly. Leo reaches for me, trying to stop me, but I push his hand aside. "Let's talk about this."

Angelo stalks across the bar, locking the front door as my father sets the gun down on the table next to him. "I can't believe this shit," Angelo hisses.

I don't know if he's referring to my father pulling a weapon in our place of business or that I got knocked up by Leo.

"How stupid can you be to pull a gun on someone in our bar?" Angelo shakes his head and answers my question like he's inside my head.

"I wasn't thinking." Papa grimaces.

Leo walks up behind me and places his hands on my shoulders, squeezing. "You should go," he tells me, like I'm going to listen.

"I'm staying," I announce. I can't trust my father and Leo alone. And not so soon after my father was willing to put a bullet in him.

Leo's grip tightens. "We'll be fine, *bella*. Let me talk to your father, man-to-man."

I peer over my shoulder at Leo. "I don't trust either of you alone."

"I'll stay," Angelo says. "I'll make sure nothing happens."

"Angelo." Leo dips his head at my brother, his old friend from when they were little.

"Leo." Angelo almost cracks a smile.

Leo turns to me and smiles softly. "Go be with your mother and let the men figure things out."

Hello, 1950s. "You can't be serious? Are you really this much of a chauvinist?"

"No, Daphne. I'm not." He shakes his head and rests his forehead against mine. "This is about respect. Respect for your family and your father. I need to talk with him and explain. It's the only way shit will work out for us."

I tip my head up so our lips are almost touching and stare into his eyes. "Okay, but tread lightly."

Even with Angelo as a middleman, things are bound to get heated. My father has never been known for his reasonable side and has always been quick to fly off the handle. I fear that leaving Leo alone with him is a recipe for disaster.

Leo kisses me softly, not lingering too long because my family's watching.

As I back away, I grab the gun off the table. "I'm taking this with me. Just in case."

Surprisingly, my father doesn't argue as I re-engage the safety and make my way toward the staircase. I look over my shoulder, staring at the three of them, hoping they can find a way to make peace.

When I turn around, my mother's sitting halfway up the staircase with her finger over her lips. "Shh," she whispers. "Sit." She motions to the step.

"What are you doing?" I ask as I squeeze in next to her.

She takes my hand in hers, intertwining our fingers. "Listening."

"But why?"

"I'll tell you later." She shakes her head, putting her index finger back in front of her mouth.

We sit in silence with our hands locked, listening to the familiar sound of chairs scraping against the hardwood floors.

"Did you do this on purpose?" my father asks Leo.

"No, Mr. Gallo. I'm not that type of man."

"I heard you were at my son's wedding. Why were you there?"

"I own the hotel," Leo says calmly, telling my father something I still can't believe.

"You do?"

"Yes. When I saw who had booked the ballroom and heard rumors you were being released, I walked into the wedding to see if you'd show up."

"Why?"

"Because even though I'm not part of my father's business, my life, along with that of my sisters', would be in danger from your newfound freedom. I needed to know if I had to beef up security."

"We've never targeted family."

"But it's easy for us to get caught in the cross fire, sir. You should know that better than anyone."

"I do. So, how did you meet my daughter?"

"We bumped into each other at the wedding."

Leo's smart enough to leave out the good stuff like

how I ended up naked in his bed or left the reception, wanting to fuck his brains out.

"And?" my father says, knowing there has to be more.

"The connection was immediate, sir. The moment I laid eyes on her, I knew I wanted her." Leo coughs, probably realizing what a stupid fucking thing that is to say to a girl's father. "I knew I wanted to get to know her better."

I grimace and look over at my mother, but she's laughing. Betty can always find the humor in the stickiest situations. I'm sure that's the only way she's been able to stay with my father as long as she has.

"Well, you certainly did that."

"I know you hate my father, but I'm asking you for your blessing. I want to be with your daughter. I want to love her. She's carrying our baby, and I want to give them the best life possible. Take care of them."

I roll my eyes, but my mother pats my hand, silently telling me to shut the fuck up.

"She doesn't need someone to take care of her, Leo. She's a strong, independent woman. She always has been and always will be. She's like her mother in that. Fiery and full of life."

I tear up a little listening to my father speak about me.

"If you think you're going to tell her what to do and run her life, you're going to get a rude awakening."

Leo's laughter fills the bar. "I've learned that about her. It may be the thing I love most about Daphne."

They're being too nice to each other. I'm sitting on the edge of the step, waiting for shit to go south. My father is being way too sweet, especially to a Conti.

"She's already pregnant, so there's nothing I can do. I can't forbid you from seeing her. What's done is done. I'm handing my business over to Johnny Marioni. Any beef I had with your father is in the past. For the sake of my grandchild, I'm willing to make amends and forget whatever bad blood we had in the past."

"You're done?" I can hear the shock in Leo's voice.

"I've spent enough time away from my family. I'm too old to go back to prison. It's a young man's game, and I don't have a taste for it anymore."

"I wish my father thought that way."

"He needs a Betty. She'll set his ass straight. I swear, if I would've been popped one more time, Betty would've skinned me alive."

I smile at my mom. Although she's nosy and over the top sometimes, I aspire to be just like her.

"I see all Gallo women are strong," Leo replies.

"But they love hard, Leo. Remember, for all of their bravado, there's a kind soul and a soft heart underneath that tough exterior. Don't mess this up, or you'll have me to deal with."

I guess this is progress. Although my father has threatened Leo again, it has nothing to do with his name and everything to do with how he treats me.

Someone should've set my father straight back in the day. He wouldn't have been a dumb shit for so many years. Maybe I was wrong. Maybe he has changed, and for once, no one will win the over-under.

CHAPTER EIGHTEEN

LEO

"I'LL BE FINE," I say to Daphne over the phone before I walk into my father's home. "Don't worry."

"That's easy for you to say. You've already had a gun pointed at you today."

I laugh. "If I can survive your father, I can survive anything."

"Your dad's going to flip."

"I know, but he'll just have to deal with his shit. It has no place in my life. If he can't, I'll choose you over him and walk away forever."

"I'd hate for that to happen."

"You don't know my father. It may be a blessing." I step onto the front stoop and take a deep breath. "I've got to run. I'll call you when I leave."

"Good luck, Leo," she says sweetly.

My father's waiting for me in the dining room, reading the newspaper and drinking espresso like he does every afternoon.

As I step into the room, he pushes his thick black glasses higher on his nose and glances up from the paper. "I'm here," he says with absolutely no warmth in his voice as he folds the paper in half and sets it off to the side. "What's so important to take you away from your work?"

I pour myself a cup of espresso, letting him stew a bit. He's watching me closely like he always does. My father's an observer. He never says much, not unless it's important to him. "You're going to be a grandfather again," I say casually, not really knowing how to start the conversation about Daphne Gallo.

"Is Alicia pregnant again?"

I laugh at how quick he rushes to judging my sisters, especially Alicia. She's thirty-five and has three children by two different men, which in my father's eyes, makes her a disgrace.

"No. Alicia's not pregnant, Pop." I lean back, holding the tiny espresso cup in one hand, hoping like hell this will go easier than I expect it to. "I'm having a baby."

My father's eyebrows rise, and it's the first time he

doesn't look angry to hear he's having another grand-child. "It's about time." He pushes his cup to the side and leans forward. "I've been waiting for you to carry on the family name."

"Well, that's the thing." I pause and sip the rich, dark espresso and revel in the taste of the old country.

"Please don't tell me you knocked up some gold-digging whore." He pinches the bridge of his nose, imagining the worst thing he can think of, but he's way off base.

"No." I shake my head. "Nothing like that."

He waves his hand over the table in circles. "Out with it, son."

"The mother is Daphne Gallo."

My father's eyes widen. He doesn't say a thing as he leans back, resting his elbow on the armrest of the chair, and he places his fingers against his lips.

"Say something."

He takes his glasses off, placing them on the table in front of him. "Santino's only daughter?"

"Yes."

"Out of all the women in Chicago, you sleep with Santino's daughter?"

"It wasn't intentional."

"Your dick just happened to fall into her?" He raises an eyebrow.

"Well, no."

"Did you know who she was when you slept with her?"

"Yes."

This is how my father works. First, he loses his shit, letting his feelings and temper get in the way of rationality. Then there're a few minutes where he rants and raves before he finally settles down. Hopefully, this won't be any different.

He slams his hand down on the table, causing the espresso pot to bounce, along with everything else, including our mugs. "How could you have been so careless?"

"Love defies logic."

"You mean your prick has no boundaries."

I stay calm because anything else could be disastrous.

"Pop, Santino's out of the business, and you two used to be friends. What's done is done. Daphne's having my child, and if you can't accept them as part of our family..."

"Wait," he says and holds up his hand. "Santino's out?"

I nod. Naturally, that's the one thing my father hears and cares about.

"This changes things," he mumbles and rubs his hands together slowly.

"You're unbelievable. Even if he weren't, it wouldn't change how I feel about Daphne or my unborn child."

"Of course not." He waves his hand dismissively. "Set up a meeting. We'll handle things."

"I'll set up a meeting, Pop, but you aren't handling anything. You either make peace, or I'm done with you," I tell him before I stand. "It's your choice. You can either gain a grandchild or lose a son."

There's nothing left to say. The ball's in my father's court now. He can continue being a hard-ass, letting business get in the way of family, or he can figure out a way to coexist with the Gallos. I'm done playing games, and I sure as hell don't live to please my father.

DAPHNE's at the bar working, when I begged her to stay home and take it easy. The woman is defiant to the core.

"What are you doing?" I ask as I sit on a barstool across from her while she dries a glass.

She stops moving and looks up at me. "Don't start."

"Did you eat today?"

"I did." Her eyes narrow.

I know she's annoyed, but I don't give a shit. I do get to voice how I feel because she's carrying my child too. "Enough?"

She sets the glass down and leans over with her elbows pressing into the bar top. "I had plenty. Is this how you're going to be the entire pregnancy?"

I shrug and play innocent. "What way is that?"

"Overbearing."

I laugh and shake my head. "I care about your well-being and our baby's. There's a difference."

"Listen," she starts to say, but then her brother walks over, stopping her from telling me off.

"Leo. Back so soon?" Angelo asks.

"I had to check on my girl."

He runs his fingers through his dark brown hair and shakes his head. "I'm not sure how I feel about you with my sister."

Daphne smacks him on the chest with the back of her hand. "Don't be a jerk, Angelo."

"You better do right by her," he tells me with a serious look. "If you don't, you won't have to worry about my father because I'll find you first."

I stare at my old childhood friend, knowing he's a man of his word just as much as I am. "Noted."

"Takes balls to come in here," Lucio, Daphne's other brother, says as he comes to stand by their side. He's staring at me more intensely, having missed the entire conversation we had earlier.

"I can't hide."

"My father's already put the word out that you're not to be touched unless provoked," Daphne says in response to Lucio's statement.

"Provoked?" I ask as I draw my eyebrows inward.

"You plannin' on drawing a gun on someone?" Lucio asks, which explains everything I need to know.

"No. I don't even carry one."

"Don't say that too loud," Angelo says and starts to laugh, but I'm not sure I see the humor.

Lucio turns his attention toward his sister. "Daphne, it's dead in here tonight. Why don't you go home and relax? You were just in the hospital yesterday, and Leo's right, you should take it easy."

"We got this," Angelo tells her and takes the towel out of her hands. "Go."

I smile, liking her brothers more than I ever expected. For once, I feel like someone is on my side instead of fighting me at every turn.

"I could go for pizza," Daphne says as she rubs her stomach.

"Pizza, it is." I smile at my girl.

"I'll grab my things. Be right back."

I watch her as she disappears down the hallway to the stock room, and when I turn around, her brothers are eyeing me.

"You break her heart, and we'll end your life," Lucio says as he leans in so no one else can hear. "If she gets hurt because of you, we'll make sure it's painful."

"And slow," Angelo adds.

I hold up my hands. "Guys, I only want to do what's right. I love your sister. I'd never do anything to hurt her, and I'd never allow anyone to put their hands on her. I'll protect her and make her happy."

"Ready?" Daphne says as she walks toward me, oblivious to what just transpired between her brothers and me.

"You two have a good night," I say as I stand and snake my arm around Daphne's back, gripping her hip.

"Let's grab the pizza and take it back to your place."

"Alfredo's?" she asks with a twinkle in her eye.

"From anywhere you want, *bella*."

Daphne devours twice as much pizza as I do, moaning the entire time.

"This is so good." She closes her eyes and hums her approval as she chews another bite. "Have you ever tasted anything better than this?"

"I have," I say, watching her carefully and trying not to let my lust overcome her hunger.

Her tongue pokes out and sweeps across her lips, and I lose all ability to think. "You're taunting me," I warn, feeling my resistance slipping.

"You look hungry," she says, giving no fucks what she's doing to me.

"I am, *bella*, and if you're not careful, I'm going to push the pizza on the floor and feast on you instead."

She gives me a smug grin. "Maybe that's all part of my master plan."

I grab the pizza slice from her fingers just as she's going for another bite. "You can eat later after we work up an appetite."

She tries to take the slice back, but I drop the piece to the floor and grab her wrists. "Me or pizza?"

"That's such a hard decision." She smirks and

moves her head from side to side like she really has to think about the answer.

"If you have to think that hard"—her gaze dips to my lips as I speak—"I need to do better."

She struggles a little in my grasp. "My answer is definitely pizza, then." She giggles.

I pull her forward, bringing her mouth close to mine. "I'm about to change your reality in a hurry, sweetheart. Be ready to never eat pizza without thinking about me again."

That's the way I want it too. I want to be her be all and end all. There's no other man in the world who'll be good enough for Daphne Gallo, and there's no way in hell I'll let another man raise my child. Daphne hasn't said yes, but she's going to be my wife.

"Such a big talker. Let's see if you have the moves to back up your words," she challenges, and I'm ready to rock her world.

I pull her into my lap and stare into her eyes. "I love you, Daphne Gallo," I whisper against her lips.

It's the first time I've said the three most important and scariest words to her. We've danced around the topic, shared our feelings, but never actually said "I love you" to one another.

She blinks slowly and smiles. "I love you too, Leo Conti. Now you better put up or shut up."

I wrap my arms around her back, pressing her body flush against mine. "Soft or hard?" I ask, giving her the choice in how she wants me to love her.

"Hard and slow," she says all breathless and wanton. She grinds her middle against my jeans. "I want to feel it tomorrow."

My lips crash down on hers as my arms tighten, holding her closer. She moans and rocks back and forth, riding my cock through the fabric of my jeans and driving me completely mindless with lust.

I want to own her body, claim her, as much as she owns mine. Her tongue dips between my lips, and I'm a goner. Daphne Gallo has me in knots, not knowing up from down or left from right.

I slide my hand up her back as she pulls my shirt up before touching my skin. She hums her approval as her fingers trace the dips and ridges of my abdomen, sending goose bumps across my chest.

My lips trace a path down her jaw, finding the spot on her neck where her heart's beating wildly, matching my own. Her knees tighten at my sides as I lick her soft skin and nibble her neck where it meets her shoulder blade. This is her magic spot. The one that makes her quiver in my arms.

Her fingers tangle in my hair as her head tips back, giving me full access. I stand as her arms wrap around my back, and my lips stay on her skin. She's in my arms, holding my face to her neck as I carry her toward the bedroom.

"I need you," she whispers as I place her on the bed and cover her body with my own.

"I want you," I say against her skin.

Her knees fall to the sides as I move down her body and unbutton her shirt, pushing the material to the sides. "Lower," she tells me.

I smile, unable to stop myself, because Daphne Gallo is always bossy. Even in bed.

She lets out a happy sigh, relaxing into the bed as I pull her pants down her legs, exposing her lace underwear. My mouth waters, and I want to be inside her, bury myself so deep I can't even breathe. But this is the part I savor, the moment I take slowly before I give her exactly what she wants...the hard stuff.

My fingers dip into the sides of her panties as I pull them down her legs and drop the clothes to the floor behind me. She lifts her ass toward my face, always impatient and a little greedy, just the way I like her.

Her knees touch the mattress as I bring my mouth down on her, sucking her clit gently. She lets out a loud gasp, jerking upward, offering her pussy to me. I take it, devouring her core with my tongue and lips, loving the way she tastes.

I'm calculated in my movements, following her body language and touching her the way she needs to be touched.

"Yes!" she cries out, rocking her bottom toward my face, practically grinding her pussy against me.

I want her orgasm. I want her pleasure. But not this way. I want to be buried deep inside her, leaving my imprint, owning her.

When my lips leave her body, her eyes fly open.

"What are you doing?" she asks as I undo my pants and kick them to the floor.

"*Bella*, I want to make love to you. I want to feel your body squeezing me, wanting me, needing me."

"But I was..."

I bring my face close to hers and stare into her eyes. "You'll come, baby. I'll make sure of it."

Her fingernails dig into the skin of my back as I push my cock ever so slowly inside her warmth. We rock together, gasping for air and never wanting the moment to end.

I make love to Daphne. First slow and loving, and then, when she's ready and I'm finally willing, I pound into her until she can't form another word.

CHAPTER NINETEEN

DAPHNE

"Are you ready for this?"

Today's the day. Our fathers have agreed to a sit-down, for a brief time, to discuss how they're going to handle our relationship and their future grandchild. They're over-the-top ridiculous and idiotic. I'll never understand why men do the crazy, silly shit they do, and age doesn't seem to help them either.

Leo leans forward and kisses the top of my head. "It'll be fine." I'm not sure if he's trying to convince me or himself.

My father wanted Mario to come to the bar for the

meeting, but we all knew that was a horrible idea. I've seen enough mafia movies to know a sit-down has to take place in a neutral location. No mob boss is willing to go into enemy territory, even if it is to call a truce.

Leo invited both men to his penthouse for a one-on-one, figuring it was the only place that made any kind of sense. He invited his father to come over early because I haven't had the pleasure, and I use that word very loosely, of meeting the Mario Conti.

"What if it's not?" I check my makeup in the mirror for at least the third time, wanting to look perfect.

I'm always a skeptic, especially when it has anything to do with my father. Leo's father is the great unknown to me, but Leo's told me he's just as much of a hard-ass as my dad. So, basically, we're screwed unless they can rise above their petty bullshit for the sake of their grandchild.

Leo squeezes my shoulders from behind me as I stare at my reflection. "Trust me. They may be pigheaded, but neither man is stupid. It's going to be all right, Daphne," he tells me when I give him a skeptical smile in the mirror.

"Why am I so nervous?"

I had trouble applying my eyeliner a few minutes ago because my hands were shaking so badly I couldn't draw a straight line to save my life. I know how much is at stake with this meeting and the myriad ways shit could go south. If my father and Mario can't work things out... Well, I don't even want to think about how that'll impact the life of my baby, *our baby*, in the future.

Before Leo can respond, the doorman calls, letting us know Mario Conti is on his way up in the elevator. I shake out my hands, trying to get rid of a little nervous energy before the show begins.

"Relax," Leo says like it's just that easy.

That's totally a man thing. My three brothers are barely ever rattled about anything. I never see them pacing with worry or popping Xanax like it's their lifeblood. That's purely a woman thing. And I'm not sexist, I'm a realist. Men let shit slide off their backs, figuring what's done is done and what will be will be, so they don't even bother spending any energy worrying about how they fucked something up. I never thought I was a worrier. But the older I get, and now with the baby on the way, my stress level is off the charts ridiculous.

The elevator chimes before the doors open, revealing an older, just as handsome version of Leo. Mr. Conti's studying something on his phone when he steps into the foyer dressed in a three-piece suit, shoes so polished I'm sure I could see my own reflection, and his hair perfectly styled like he just stepped out of the silver fox edition of *GQ* magazine.

His gaze travels up my body, but not in that creepy way, before his eyes meet mine. There's no smile on his face, no way for me to judge what the hell he's thinking.

"Pop, it's good of you to join us," Leo says, greeting his father with way more formality than I've ever greeted mine.

His father's eyes veer away from me for a moment to look at his son, and I'm thankful for a reprieve, even if it's short-lived. "Leo," he says coldly before his gaze is back on me. "You must be Daphne." He steps forward, entering the foyer which now seems way too small for the three of us.

"It's nice to meet you, Mr. Conti." I somehow smile, even though all I want to do is run and hide.

He studies me for a moment, not saying a word. I'm about to hyperventilate, wishing I could excuse myself and slink away to anywhere else but here. "I can see why my son is so enamored of you," he tells me, finally cracking what I think is a smile.

I glance nervously to Leo for a moment, looking for a rescue. "Thank you, sir." I keep my words formal, always remembering my upbringing and the respect for my elders that was practically beaten into me as a child.

"Mario, please." He dips his chin and takes another step closer.

I resist the urge to back up and flee, knowing it'll do nothing to help smooth the waters and gain favor with Leo's father. "Mario," I say softly.

Mario grabs my hand and lifts it to his mouth.

"You've grown into a beautiful woman, Daphne." He kisses the top of my hand so softly, I barely feel his lips on my skin.

Sometimes I forget the Contis lived in our neighborhood. I can't remember a time when there was peace in my life instead of the constant bullshit my father has brought on my family over the last two decades.

Leo pulls me backward as Mario releases my hand. "Would you like some coffee, Pop?" Leo asks as he moves us toward the living room like he's trying to put distance between his father and me.

"I'll take a glass of wine," Mario answers as he follows behind us to the living room.

"Thanks for coming today," I say out of nervousness as I place a hand on my stomach. "It means a lot to us."

Mario takes a seat on the couch across from me, studying my face with his steely eyes. "We're going to be family," Leo's father says a few moments later.

I nod and tug at the hem of my skirt, pulling it down over my knees. "We are." I laugh for some reason, wishing I could have a glass of wine too. Awkward moments are always easier to swallow with a drink.

Mario takes the glass of wine from Leo, looking every bit a businessman instead of a cold-hearted mobster. There's a not-so-comfortable silence as we sit on the couch, Leo and I on one side of the room, and his father on the other. In situations like this, I always talk, trying to fill the void. Silence isn't something I'm used to in my family. Three brothers and a very outspoken mom make quiet almost an impossibility.

"Leo told me you already have grandchildren," I say, trying to find middle ground for us to discuss.

"Ah, yes." He lifts his wineglass to his lips and pauses. "Alicia's always been a problem child."

Alicia is one of Leo's sisters, and from everything I've heard about her, she is, in fact, a problem. If I didn't know the backstory, I would've been taken aback by Mario's comment about his daughter. But knowing what I know, and her propensity to bed-hop, I know his father can't exactly be proud of her antics.

"Pop," Leo warns. "Be nice."

"I love my grandchildren. I couldn't cherish their little faces any more than I already do, but my daughter..." He shakes his head and sighs. "She's always taken a different path and not one I would've chosen for her."

Mario is trying to be civil. From the way Leo described him, his father is putting his best foot forward as we sit in the living room, waiting for my father. I replace Alicia's name in his sentence and know he's not exactly thrilled about the path Leo took either. I'm sure when he pictured his son having his own children, it wasn't with the daughter of his mortal enemy.

Mario leans forward and places his wineglass on

the coffee table which separates us. "Can I speak freely?" he asks as he rests his elbows on his legs near his knees, looking at us over the frame of his black glasses.

"Of course," I say, not letting Leo answer first. "I'm never one to bullshit, Mario."

"When I heard about you and my son, I wasn't exactly happy." Mario rubs his hands together in front of himself and glances down at the hardwood floor for a second. "But the way my son looks at you is much the same way I looked at his mother before she agreed to be my wife. Nothing and no one could've said anything to change my feelings for her."

I don't say anything as I peer over at Leo, who is, in fact, staring at me. I'm not sure there's anything I could actually say in response to Mario's statement, so I decide to keep my mouth shut and just listen for once.

"My approval is not needed, but I give it willingly," he says. "I only want the best for my son's first child."

There's a little misogyny in his words. I hear the sexism plain as day. There's something about the males in Italian families having their own children that always earns favor above everyone else.

"I will do my best to work things out with your father. For the sake of my unborn grandchild and the future of our families."

This is progress.

Leo's phone dings, and he glances down. "Your

father is here," he tells me, covering my hand with his and squeezing.

Mario stands as Leo does, but I beat them to the elevator doors. I want my face to be the first one my father sees as he steps foot in Leo's penthouse.

"Papa," I say as soon as I see my father. He's pulled out all the stops, looking every bit as dapper as Mr. Conti in a three-piece suit and newly polished shoes.

My father's never been one for suits. He's worn them, but usually only for funerals and weddings. I can't tell which category this meeting falls into. Probably a little bit of both. One part of his life is ending, and a new chapter is about to begin.

When my father wraps his arms around me, I feel him stiffen as Mario walks behind me. "Be good today," I remind Papa. "This is for the baby, not your ego."

He kisses my cheeks as he backs away and smiles. "I know how to handle men like Mario," he tells me, and that's exactly what I'm afraid of.

I want them to bury the hatchet, but I don't even know if it's possible with all the bad blood between them. Years of turf wars, murder, and backstabbing make the possibility of a truce pretty close to impossible. These two men have to rise above their work for the sake of their children and unborn grandchild.

"Santino," Mario says as my father releases me.

My father dips his head. "Mario."

Well, this is a start. They've been in the same room

for thirty seconds, and there hasn't been any bloodshed.

Baby steps. This is good.

Leo wraps his arm around my back and grips my hip roughly. "Let's go into the living room, shall we?" Leo says to both men as they stare each other down.

I take a step and immediately double over like someone just sucker-punched me in the gut.

"Daphne," Leo says, his voice filled with panic.

My hand flies to my stomach, and I gasp for air, feeling like someone's trying to rip my uterus out through my belly button.

"Something's wrong."

CHAPTER TWENTY

LEO

"I'm sure she'll be fine," my father says as he stands across from me in the waiting room.

I pace, wearing a path into the off-white linoleum. "I can't believe they won't let me back there."

The nurse practically shoved me out of the emergency room, telling me they had to run tests and I should go relax in the waiting room while they evaluated Daphne and the baby.

"There was a time when they wouldn't even allow men in the delivery room for the birth of their child.

Remember?" My father asks Santino, trying to be friendlier than I've seen him in years.

"Life was easier then," Santino tells him. "Much simpler."

Besides our fathers' small talk, the only other sound in the waiting room is the tap of my dress shoes on the tile. I cross the entire room in seven quick steps, before spinning on my heels and repeating. I can't sit still. I can't chitchat and talk about the good old days.

I glance at my watch, wondering what the hell is going on. It's been an hour since they wheeled her to the back, and there's been no news or updates as I was promised.

I walk up to the reception desk and scan the surface, looking for anything with Daphne's name on it.

"Can I help you, sir?" the nurse asks as soon as she looks up from the computer screen.

"I'm here with Daphne Gallo. Are there any updates on her condition?"

She taps a few keys and shakes her head. "The system hasn't been updated yet, but I'm sure a doctor will be out soon to talk to you."

Her words don't give me any solace. I'm not used to sitting on the sidelines, waiting for updates.

"Leo," Mr. Gallo says as he walks out of the waiting room and comes to stand at my side. "You have to calm down. I know it's hard." He grabs my shoulders and stares me in the eyes. "Daphne needs you to be strong and not lose your shit. You hear me?"

I nod and clench my fists tightly at my sides. "I'll be strong, Mr. Gallo. But until I know she's all right, I can and will lose my shit."

"Daphne's a fighter," he tells me, trying to put my mind at ease.

"Mr. Conti," a woman says, standing in the doorway separating the emergency room from the rest of the hospital.

"Here." I blow out a breath and walk toward her. "Can I see her now?"

She nods. "Only one person for right now, and Ms. Gallo is asking for you."

Mr. Gallo shoos me forward. "Go. Be with her. We'll be waiting for you. Your father and I aren't going anywhere."

I follow the nurse down a long corridor of what seems like endless rooms filled with moaning patients and annoying beeping monitors. "She's resting now." The nurse motions toward the door. "The doctor will be in soon to give you an update."

My footsteps are quiet as I walk into the room, trying not to wake her. Her eyes are closed, and her hands are covering her stomach in a protective way as she lies on the gurney, covered in a thin white blanket. I slide onto the chair next to her, scared to touch her and doing my best to let her rest.

"Leo," she whispers and moves her hand to her side. "They won't tell me anything."

"Shh, *bella*." I grab her hand, squeezing it tightly. "The doctor's coming."

"What if something's wrong?" I can hear the panic in her voice.

"Everything will be fine," I lie because it's easier for me to believe that everything will work out. "I know it will be."

A doctor walks in, looking no older than a high school kid, and studies a folder of papers. "Ms. Gallo," he says before looking up at us.

"Yes." I answer for her.

He flips another page, drawing out the agony and oblivious to our terror. "First off, the baby's perfectly healthy."

I finally exhale, feeling relieved and like a weight has been lifted off my shoulders. "Were you under any stress when you started cramping?"

"A little," she says as she pulls herself upright a bit more on the gurney.

A little stress is sitting in traffic on the Kennedy when you're late for a meeting. What just happened in my penthouse rises to the level of a red alert during the Cold War.

"You're going to need to cut down on your stress as soon as possible. Also, add some fiber to your diet. You're constipated, which made the cramping worse than normal."

I laugh, covering my mouth with my free hand.

Daphne shoots me a death glare. "That's funny?" she asks and lets out a sarcastic laugh. "Ha-ha. I'm constipated."

"*Bella.*" I lean forward and press my lips to her forehead. "I always knew you were full of shit, but now the doctor's confirmed it."

She swats my arm, not feeling the same sense of playful relief I am. "Thank you, Doctor."

He closes the folder in his hands and tucks it under his arm. "Maybe take it easy for a few weeks just to be safe."

"I'll make sure she rests," I tell him because I won't allow Daphne to put her life at risk as well as our baby's.

"The discharge nurse will be here soon."

"Can I get dressed?" she asks before he has a chance to walk out the door.

"Yes, but get up slowly."

Daphne blows out a breath and rolls her eyes.

I know this taking-it-easy lifestyle isn't going to sit well with her. I'm going to have to find ways to make her relax and be creative about it. If she thinks I'm handling her in any way, I'll be fucked.

She starts to sit up, and I grab her by the shoulders. "What are you doing?" Her eyes narrow as she glances down at my hands.

"Nothing," I say quickly, but I don't pull away. "I'm just helping you."

"I'm not broken."

I tighten my grip when she tries to push my hands away. "For the good of the baby."

Those are the magic words because she instantly stops fighting me. "Fine," she mutters and motions for her clothes. "Only because I don't want anything to happen to our baby."

As she gets dressed, I ask a passing nurse to bring our fathers in while we wait for her discharge. I know they acted nonchalant about everything, but they were worried too.

"Daphne," Mr. Gallo says as he rushes into the room and sees Daphne standing and fully dressed. "Is everything okay?"

My father's behind him. "Is the baby okay?"

"Everything's fine," I tell them both, but I leave out the bit about her being constipated. "She needs to avoid stress. Today was too much for her."

"I'm sorry," my father says.

I raise my eyebrows because that may very well be the first time I've ever heard him apologize. "Both of you need to work your shit out before it affects our baby, your grandchild." I punctuate the last word, reminding them a part of each of them is growing inside her.

"Yes. Yes. Of course," Mr. Gallo says and glances at my father. "We talked in the waiting room. Whatever's in the past will stay there."

"Son." My father puts his hand on my shoulder.

"Santino is telling you the truth. We've buried the hatchet."

I eye him skeptically.

"For the good of our grandchild," he adds.

"What about Johnny?" I ask, knowing he's taking over for Santino and there's bound to be some carryover.

"I've arranged a sit-down. We'll iron things out. The city's big enough for all of us."

Daphne looks at me and is just as shocked as I am that they sound like grown-ups about the entire situation. Our entire lives, we've listened to these two men trash-talk the other, ready to fight to the death.

Even though they're being overly friendly, I imagine there will come a day when the competition kicks in. Whether it be Christmas or birthdays, the other isn't going to be the cheap grandpa, giving shitty gifts. I'm fine with it. Let them spoil our baby and shower him or her with gifts.

"I'm taking Daphne away for a little while," I say.

"You are?" Daphne glares at me. "We didn't discuss anything, sweetheart." She pulls a tight smile, barely moving her lips as she speaks.

"We could both use some time away."

"I can't leave my brothers short-handed at the bar."

"I'll take care of your shifts," her father responds quickly.

Daphne's head snaps back to him. "Papa, come on."

He puts his hands up. "I'll do it. I'm retired now and have extra time on my hands. Besides, I want you to make sure my grandbaby is healthy."

"Our grandbaby," my father corrects him as the rivalry heats up, only in a new and different way.

"I don't know," she says and glances at the floor.

I place my fingers under her chin, bringing her eyes to mine. "They can handle it."

"Okay," she whispers, finally giving in.

CHAPTER TWENTY-ONE

DAPHNE

THE SUN WARMS my face as we sit at a charming little café in the middle of the town square. Mountains stand tall behind the buildings as if they're reaching for heaven, not realizing they are already set in paradise.

After a month in Italy, my ability to speak the language of my ancestors is still atrocious. Leo's been my saving grace, translating like he was born here.

"I could live here forever," I say, tipping my head back to soak up a little more sun.

Life is slow here. There's no rushing from one place to the next, no traffic jams or police sirens at all hours of the night. The quaint little village of Castel di Sangro, tucked in a valley between the lush mountains and Leo's great-grandparents' hometown, is exactly how I imagined the old country to be.

"We could buy a place and raise the baby here," he says as he lifts the espresso cup to his lips.

I glance at him and shake my head. "I can't leave my family. I need my mom most of all, especially with the baby coming." I touch the tiny bump that's finally starting to grow, making the pregnancy all too real.

"We can spend summers here at the very least."

I nod, liking the idea, because I can't imagine anything better than escaping the loud, harsh city for the green countryside so filled with history and peace.

"See that church?" Leo motions across the square to a three-story white building which has seen better days. "My great-grandparents were married there, as their parents were."

I study him because Leo doesn't make small talk or drop useless information unless he's going somewhere with it. "That's so sweet." I smile, taking in the beauty of the old structure.

"I was wondering," he says as he places his cup back on the table and grasps my hand. "What do you think about getting married there?"

"Okay," I say quickly.

"Because the baby will be here soon, and I'd love to..." He pauses, and his eyebrows draw together when my response finally registers. "Wait. What?"

"I said okay," I repeat, knowing he wasn't expecting me to say yes.

Leo's face relaxes as a smile spreads across his handsome face. "I thought I'd have to fight you on this."

I shake my head, knowing it's exactly how I want our family to start. Steeped in history and tradition, surrounded by love and joy. "It's perfect."

He stands up and takes my hand, pulling me into his arms. "You've made me the happiest man in the world, *bella*."

I peer up, staring into those sinful honey-brown eyes that captured me not that long ago. "I want us to be a family, Leo, in every sense of the word."

He leans forward and presses his lips to mine, stealing my breath like he does every time he kisses me. I wrap my arms around his middle and hold him tight, wishing we could stay like this forever.

"How about tomorrow?" he asks.

"Tomorrow, what?"

His embrace tightens. "We'll get married tomorrow."

"That's too soon. I need—" I start to say when he cuts me off.

"Your family is already on the way here. I have an appointment set for you at the dress shop in town, and the rings are already being made."

I blink a few times, totally in shock. "How?"

He's barely left my side this entire trip. How he had time to pull together a wedding, including flying my family to Italy, is beyond me. I've barely had the energy to make it to sunset every night without taking at least one catnap.

"While you sleep," he says and brushes his lips against mine.

"Oh, well," I mumble. "Tomorrow."

I try to let that sink in. Tomorrow, I'll no longer be Daphne Gallo, I'll be Daphne Conti. I wonder how Leo would feel if I decided to hyphenate my name, but that conversation can wait until another day.

"A marriage license. We need one."

"Taken care of, and this is about saying our vows before God more than the law."

Then there's no rush to discuss the legalities of which last name I'll use. I push it to the side, not wanting to ruin this perfect day.

"When does my family land?"

"Your mom is meeting you at the dress shop, and your brothers and father are already back at the hotel."

"What about your father?"

"He's at the hotel too."

I'm speechless. Somehow while we've been gone, our fathers have avoided killing each other and kept the truce in place without our having to step in the middle and remind them of their promise. It's like a modern-day miracle.

Leo places his hands on the sides of my face and stares at me. "I love you, Daphne. I want this day to be perfect. I want you to remember it always."

"I will." I rest my forehead against his lips, loving the way his hands feel on me and riding high on cloud nine.

My mother squeals as soon as we walk in the front door of the quaint little dress shop near the café. She rushes toward me with her arms open. I run to her, forgetting about Leo for a second because I've missed my mom more than anyone this month.

"Mama," I say, holding her so tight both of us can barely breathe.

"Baby, I've missed you so much." She buries her face in my hair like she used to do when I was a little girl. "You look so happy."

"I am," I whisper in her ear and squeeze her one more time before finally letting go.

"Mrs. Gallo," Leo says as he stands behind me.

My mother pushes me out of the way and tackle-hugs the man, practically knocking him over. "I'm a hugger," she tells him like he hasn't figured that one out yet.

"Well, good thing for you, I like to be hugged." He laughs and peers at me over my mother's head because she's a good foot shorter than him.

"It's so nice to see you again." She backs away and touches his chest. "And for such a happy occasion no less."

I swear she's kneading his pecs, totally feeling him up. Leo doesn't seem to mind. He's standing still, letting her touch him. "I'm just glad Daphne said yes."

"That would've been awkward." My mother glances over her shoulder at me. "Has she been taking it easy?" she whispers.

"I can hear you."

"Oh." She starts to laugh.

I pull my mother away from Leo's chest. "I've been taking it easy. Leo's made sure of it."

"We better get started. We don't have much time, and you have a lot of dresses to try on."

"She could wear a bag, and she'd be beautiful," Leo tells my mother before he kisses my cheek. "Spare no expense, *bella*. Buy anything you want."

My mother starts to clap. "A man after my own heart," she says, staring at Leo like he's Prince Charming. "Now, go. You can't see the dress." She shoos him toward the door.

"Have fun, ladies," Leo tells us before he leaves us alone.

"Tell me he has some major flaw."

"Ma." I give her a look.

"What? I may be old, but I'm sure as hell not dead."

"Soon, we'll be picking out your dress," I remind her, wondering what the hell happened to their wedding plans.

"Your father wants to elope to Vegas and be married by an Elvis impersonator." She rolls her eyes.

"Vegas could be fun."

"An ex-mobster in a gangster town is not a smart combo, dear."

"Yeah." I forgot about Vegas's illustrious roots, and with my father's sudden departure from his previous life, it most definitely could be a recipe for disaster.

"We'll get married at the bar and invite the neighborhood." She waves her hands toward the dresses. "I don't need all this after being together for more than three decades."

I'll have to plant the bug in my father's ear. My mother deserves something grand for putting up with his shit for all these years. I wouldn't have stuck around, waiting for him to grow up and praying every night he didn't end up in the county morgue.

"You're never too old for romance, Ma."

I GAZE at Leo as we stand on the altar of the old church, surrounded by our family in an intimate ceremony. The priest is Italian, speaking only a few words of broken English, but it doesn't matter.

"You look beautiful," Leo mouths as the priest says a prayer over our rings, blessing them along with our union.

I picked the dress just for him, wanting to knock his socks off with something classy. The bottom of the silk gown pools at my feet and hugs my body in all the right places, even showing off the baby bump perfectly.

Leo's dressed in a black suit and silver tie, looking every bit as delicious as the night we met. That's how we ended up in this situation. Me pregnant, and him begging me to be his forever.

My mother sniffles from the first row, always the first one to cry at a wedding. I couldn't have planned a better wedding myself. I don't need the flashy reception and hundreds of guests to profess my love and devotion to my future husband and baby's father.

I've learned a lot about Leo, myself, and life during our trip away from our hectic lives in the city. Life's sweet and short, needing to be savored like a fine wine instead of chugged like a cheap beer. Italy has helped me realize that. There's no rush to be anywhere, meals are an event instead of a necessity, and everything has to do with pleasure.

In Chicago, everything is fast-paced, hectic, and anxiety-ridden. But now, after so long away, I crave the easiness of the tiny villages lined with cobblestone streets which scatter out like a spider web from the center.

Last night after dinner, I told Leo I'd be slowing down when we returned. I know he thought I was joking, but there's no way I want to go back to the insanity of running a business when I don't have to. I'll pitch in, but my late-night shifts five days a week are a thing of the past. I want to be the mom who stays home with her baby, cuddling him or her and spoiling them rotten just like my mother did with us.

Memories are our legacy. We're not remembered for how many hours we worked or the size of our bank account. Our actions are our imprint on people's souls. How we treat others, the time we spend listening, and the way we love deeply are what will stay with a person long after we're gone. I want the memories to be sustaining, lasting well beyond my lifetime. I want to be remembered for touching their souls and leaving a lasting imprint on their hearts.

I want my friends, family, and baby to think of me for the love I showered on them and not for the time I spent chained to a neighborhood bar on the South Side of Chicago.

I want my legacy to be undeniable.

EPILOGUE

DAPHNE

Seven Months Later

"Breathe," Leo says, pushing the damp hair away from my forehead. "Remember Lamaze."

I growl and grit my teeth, wondering how I ever loved the man who put me in this situation. "I'm fucking breathing," I howl as the next contraction hits, catching me off guard.

I want to rip his face off. Scratch that, I want to rip his dick off, so this can never happen to me again.

There's no amount of classes or books that can prepare someone for labor. My body feels like it's slowly ripping in half, and there's nothing I can do to take the pain away.

Leo exhales through his mouth, sucking in a quick breath, like I'm going to do the same because there isn't a watermelon trying to come out of my cunt.

"Shut the fuck up," I hiss and push his face away, sick of listening to him.

"*Bella*, don't be that way. This is such a happy day."

"For who?" I yell, snarling at the man I showered with kisses when we woke up this morning. "You're not dying. I am."

Maybe I'm being a martyr, but every mother going through labor deserves to be whatever the hell she wants to be because the pain is immense.

I'm not talking about just a little bit. Take the worst pain you've ever experienced, magnify it by twenty, and stretch it across so many hours, you pray for death.

That's birth.

"You're being a little overdramatic."

The nurse looks over, knowing my mood went from bad to shit in under a half a millisecond.

"Leo, if I live through this, I'm going to make you pay."

"Come on. You love me," he says and tries to lean in and kiss my cheek.

I turn my head, not wanting anything to do with his lips. "So. Help. Me. God."

"How's it going?" my mother asks, bringing me a new plastic cup filled with ice chips and oblivious to the carnage that's about to take place.

"She's thinking of all the ways she can off me," Leo tells her with a small laugh like he doesn't actually think I'm serious.

"Don't laugh, kiddo. The hate is real at this stage," my mom says and shakes her head. "It's like cornering a wild bear while covered in honey. You're liable to get mauled."

Leo backs up a step, glancing down at me in shock. "Well, I..."

"She blames you for this." My mother waves her hand over my belly. "It'll take her a while before she can ever look at you the same way again."

"I'm right here," I say because they're talking about me like I'm not even in the room.

I know my mom's only trying to help. How the hell she did this four times is beyond me. I can't see myself willingly doing this again, no matter how cute the kid grows up to be.

My mother hands me the ice chips, but all I really want is a large pizza covered in pepperoni and dripping with grease.

"Thanks, Ma." I try to muster a smile.

My insides are twisting again like I'm being torn apart by the baby's fingernails one layer at a time. "You did this shit four times," I say to my mother when I can finally breathe again. "How? Why?"

She takes my hand in hers and smiles sweetly. "When you lay eyes on your baby and fall head over heels in love, you forget the pain."

I laugh cynically. "I will never forget this pain. Never."

"Sweetheart," she says softly. "All the happy memories and years you've given me have released every second of agony you put me through when I was in labor. And I mean, it was hell on earth. Epidurals were still too new when you were born for me to get one without worry."

"I'm dying, Ma," I groan.

"Don't be a drama queen. In the olden days..."

"Don't tell me people squatted in a field, had the baby, and kept on working. I don't want to hear it."

Leo collapses in a chair next to my bed, looking more disheveled than I've ever seen him before. His hair's messy, the first three buttons on his dress shirt are undone, and his tie is loose and hanging around his neck.

"Well, if you're anything like me, sweetheart, you won't be in labor much longer."

Pain slices through me again as every muscle in my abdomen tightens. I gasp, trying to breathe to alleviate some of the pain, but nothing seems to help.

"Are we ready to see how far along you are?" the

doctor asks as he walks into the room, looking way too cheerful for me.

"Get this baby out of me," I tell him. If I could reach down and pull the baby out myself, I'd do it in a heartbeat. Anything to make the pain stop.

The doctor puts on a pair of gloves and sits down between my legs. "Have you thought any more about an epidural?"

I had always said I wanted to do natural childbirth, using the techniques of Lamaze. I thought I was a hard-ass and could take pain better than most people...which is ridiculous. I was obviously delusional.

"I want one as soon as possible. I can't take the pain much longer."

"Well, let's get in there."

By there, he means my vagina. The thing I used to love, and so did Leo. Now, it's a bringer of pain and giver of life. My poor pussy will never be the same. Permanently destroyed by the tiny human trying to rip me apart from the inside.

"Just relax," the doctor says before he practically shoves his entire arm up my cunt, feeling out my cervix. "You're dilated enough for an epidural."

"Give it to me now," I say without hesitation. I'm no longer looking to be a tough chick. There's no medal of honor for enduring the pain. The kid's not going to be the least bit impressed when they get older because I went to hell and back just so they could be born.

"Are you sure?" Leo asks, still sitting in his chair, pain-free and a lucky son of a bitch he's still breathing.

I point at him and narrow my gaze. "You shut your mouth." I would've lunged off the bed and wrapped my hands around his neck if I weren't tethered to the doctor because his hand's still up my twat.

Leo throws his hands in the air, maybe realizing the precarious position he's in. "Anything you want, *bella*."

My mother laughs and shakes her head. "Don't argue with her, Leo."

"I'd never." He shakes his head, learning not to fight me on anything because I'll just dig my heels in more. "I think an epidural is a great idea."

The doctor snaps his gloves off and stands. "The anesthesiologist will be in shortly to administer the epidural. You'll feel better once it's in place and doing its job."

"Thank fuck," I hiss.

"You're about seven centimeters dilated. We're almost there."

I don't know why everyone in the room keeps referring to my birth as a we. I'm the only one in excruciating pain. The only one about to give birth. There's no we about it. Everybody else is just an observer of my misery and not an active participant.

I groan and writhe around with each passing contraction, waiting for the epidural to arrive and wondering what the hell birth is really going to be like.

The kid's still in my uterus and hasn't even started the slow and mighty tight trip down to my vagina. I think of the shoulders and cringe, knowing the real pain hasn't even begun.

A few minutes later, the anesthesiologist walks into the room with some paperwork and the biggest needle I've ever seen in my life. "Are we ready for some relief?" he asks, being chipper like everybody else who walks into my room.

"Never been so ready for something in my entire life," I say as the nurse scans my medical bracelet.

"You'll feel better quick," he says, setting every-thing out on a tray next to my bed. "You're going to need to sit up so I can get at your back."

Sitting up, or should I say, the act of sitting up, has become damn near impossible. My stomach's the size of a beach ball, and I don't even remember what my feet look like anymore.

Leo rushes to my side as I try to pull myself up and fail. I don't push him away or try to claw his face off because I need him to help me make this pain go away.

Leo pulls me up, and I throw my legs over the side. I have no shame left as everyone in this room has seen either my ass or my pussy. It's no longer sacred or pretty either.

"The nurse is going to help me navigate your contractions, so we can do this safely." He's doing something to my back as he speaks, but I don't bother to ask. All I want is relief, and whatever it takes to make that happen, I'll do. "You need to hold completely still while I do this procedure."

I don't even remember what it's like to be still. The pain and aftermath of each passing contraction make me move around the bed like I'm drunk dancing on the floor, too plastered to stand on my own two feet.

Leo looks me straight in the eye, holding my arms with each hand as he lowers himself so we're face-to-face. "Just look at me," he says.

I level him with my gaze. "You're the reason I'm in this much pain."

"I know. Focus on your hate," he tells me. "Plot my death in your head if you must. Just stay still."

My fingernails dig into his arms as I clutch him while he's holding on to me. The procedure's quicker than I imagined and not nearly as painful because, again, there's a human ripping out of my body.

"In a few minutes, you'll feel numb," the anesthesiologist says. "You can lie back down and relax."

"You're doing great," Leo says sweetly.

I still want to rip his face off, but the need to do so lessens every few seconds.

The nurse presses a few buttons on the fetal monitor as I lie back down. "You should be able to get some rest now. You're going to need it for delivery."

My mother stands at the foot of my bed and smiles. "I'm going to go talk to your father and brothers. I'll be back, sweetheart. Sleep a little."

"Yeah, Ma. I'll do my best."

Moments later, everyone's gone, and it's just Leo and me left in the room.

"Better?" he asks.

"Maybe," I say, but I can already feel the epidural working its magic, reducing the agony.

Leo leans over the bed and grabs my hand. "Just rest, *bella*."

I close my eyes, thinking I can get a few hours. But I should've known better. Hospitals are not the place for any type of relaxation. People are constantly in and out of the room, staring up my birth canal like it holds some magical answers to the universe. There's a flurry of people, studying my vital signs and the baby's heartbeat. There's no rest. There will never be a moment's peace for the rest of my entire life because I'm about to be a mother.

"Push," the doctor says as I hold my knees, feeling more exhausted than I have ever felt in my entire life.

"You can do this," Leo cheers me on, and I'm back to wanting to end his life.

I feel like I'm attempting to take the biggest shit of my life, and no matter how hard I try to bear down and push it out, there's nothing moving.

"I can see the head," the doctor says, looking up from between my legs.

"Get the baby out of me," I plead as tears stream

down my face, pushing with everything I have in me.

"Just a few more pushes," the doctor says, like that's going to make me feel any better.

I don't want to do a few more pushes. Hell, I don't even want to do one more. I want this all to be over, holding the baby in my arms, forgetting all about the last twelve hours of my life.

"You're doing so well." Leo smiles as he wipes down my face with a cool, damp cloth.

"How about you two grab her legs and help her through the last few?" the doctor tells Leo and my mother, and I know we're about to get to the grand finale.

Each one of them holds a knee, staring between my legs as I pull myself forward and push with everything I've got.

The doctor urges, "Harder, harder, more, keep going."

The hate I felt for Leo transfers to the man huddled between my legs, telling me to do something I'm doing my best at already to push the baby out.

The pain's gone, replaced by the most intense pressure of my life. I would've straight up died without the epidural. I know that now.

Three pushes later, I gasp for air as the baby's shoulders break free.

"Oh my God," my mother says as tears form in her eyes, and she covers her mouth.

"*Bella,*" Leo says, staring between my legs like he's

seen the most beautiful sight.

I press my head into the pillow, feeling relieved to have survived the delivery and happy as hell to have it over.

"Congratulations," the doctor says, holding the baby in his arms before placing it on my chest. "You have a son."

Leo wipes his face, hiding the tears I have no doubt are falling fast. "A son," he whispers.

"Would you like to cut the umbilical cord?" the doctor asks Leo.

"Yes." Leo nods.

Tears stream down my face, matching my mother and Leo, but for entirely different reasons. I'm happy, for sure, but my tears of joy are that the birth is over. The baby howls as the harsh realities of life slam down on both of us.

I'm a mother.

There's no going back, only forward.

THE ENTIRE FAMILY, including Leo's father, squeezed into my hospital room as soon as the nurse said it was okay to have visitors. They jockeyed for position like it was a contest, leaving Mr. Conti and Leo on one side and my mother and father on the other. Delilah, Lucio, Vinnie, Angelo, and Michelle filled in the gap, closing off a circle of people I never thought I'd see crammed into such a tiny space...well, at least not without some sort of bloodshed.

The way they're gawking at the little guy in my arms, it's like they've never seen a baby before.

"He's so beautiful," my mother says as she rests her head against my father's shoulder.

"Look at all that hair. Just like you, Leo," Mario tells Leo. He's even a little choked up but hides it well. Lord forbid he show the heart underneath his steely mob boss exterior.

"You two have been keeping his name a secret for months. What is it?" my father asks.

I smile at Leo, knowing this has bothered our families, but we still didn't give in. To be honest, we had a few names picked out and couldn't decide, leaving the decision until we actually laid eyes on our little boy.

"We're paying respect to our grandfathers," Leo announces as he squeezes my hand and looks around the room. "His name is Nino Raffaele Conti."

"It's perfect." My mother wipes the tears which have started to fall a little harder and easier than before.

"It's a fine name," Mario says. "Strong."

My mother takes Nino from my arms, and the attention goes with him.

"How are you feeling?" Delilah asks.

"Like roadkill." I laugh.

"Yeah. That feeling doesn't go away for a while. First, it's physical and then it's mental, but," Delilah says and looks up at Leo, "at least you have someone to help you with the newborn."

I can't imagine going through any of this alone. Delilah's obviously a much stronger person than I am because I would've been a total hot mess without the support of my family and my husband.

"You're a rock star, Delilah."

"Oh, stop," she says and blushes. "I can't imagine doing it alone again."

"Again?" I tilt my head and raise an eyebrow.

She places one hand over her stomach and winks. "Don't tell," she mouths.

I had wondered why Lucio seemed happier than usual, and now it makes total sense. With the way he loves Lulu, I know he's going to be over the moon experiencing all the joys and horrors from the beginning.

"Since we're all here," my father says and clears his throat. "Your mother and I have an announcement."

The room goes silent.

"We set a date," my mother explains.

I roll my eyes. It's been almost a year since my father announced they were getting married, and in typical Santino fashion...there was absolutely no hurry.

My father pulls my mother close. "We're getting married on December 23rd."

"Way to go, Pop," Vinnie says as he punches my father in the shoulder, almost knocking him over.

"It's about fucking time," Angelo adds.

"Are you sure about this?" Lucio asks my mother

and somehow keeps a straight face.

"He's finally going to make an honest woman out of me." My mother laughs. "It only took four kids and four grandkids, but it's finally happening."

The normal life I craved not too long ago has finally become my new reality. Happy family, sexy husband, beautiful baby, and for once, everyone is getting along...even with Mario, which is a miracle in itself.

I shift in my bed, finding it damn near impossible to get comfortable because my poor body has just been through battle. Anyone who says otherwise is being a goddamn martyr.

"Maybe we should go," Angelo tells my family when he glances down at the bed, and we lock eyes as I grimace.

"No, no. I'm fine," I say, trying to play it off because I never like to look weak.

"You're right, Ang. I'm sure Leo and Daphne would like some time alone," Lucio says.

Vinnie walks up to the side of the bed and kisses my cheek. "I love you, sis. You should've named him Vinnie, but I totally understand. He would've had some big shoes to fill."

"Shut up," I say, trying not to laugh because everything in my body hurts. "Get out of here."

My father's phone rings, and he turns his back to us as he answers. "Yeah?" There's a short pause before my father's shoulders slump forward. "When?

Where?" All eyes are on my dad as he turns around. "I have to go," he says and walks toward me. "I'm sorry."

"What's wrong?" I ask because he's tense and all traces of happiness he had moments ago are gone.

"Don't worry about it, sweetheart." My father kisses my cheek and brushes my hair away from the side of my face. "Enjoy my new grandson. I'll be back to check on you later."

"Pop." Angelo takes a step toward our father before he has a chance to leave. "What happened?"

My father's pale. The only other time I saw him like this was when he was about to be arrested. "Are you being arrested?" I ask, jumping to the only conclusion that makes sense.

Vinnie places his hand on my father's shoulder and squeezes. "Just tell us, Pop."

My father faces Mario, staring him straight in the eyes. "Johnny's been shot."

And the serenity and normalcy I thought I finally had disappears.

The Men of Inked: Southside series continues in Hook, book three! Hustle is now available for preorder everywhere!

Angelo will steal your heart!

PREORDER

Men of Inked: Southside 3
by visiting **chellebliss.com/hook**

Want a **TEXT MESSAGE** when Hook releases?
Text **GALLOS** to **24587**
(US & Canada Only... Sorry!)

If you haven't met the original Men of Inked, pick up
Men of Inked Boxset for **FREE** on all retailers!
Visit chellebliss.com/free

I hope you love Leo & Daphne! Feel free to drop me a
line and let me know your thoughts.
authorchellebliss@gmail.com

COMING IN THE MEN OF INKED:
SOUTHSIDE SERIES

visit **chellebliss.com/southside** for information.

PREORDER HOOK
Men of Inked: Southside 3
by visiting *chellebliss.com/hook*

ABOUT CHELLE BLISS

Chelle Bliss is the *USA Today* bestselling author of the Men of Inked and ALFA P.I. series. She hails from the Midwest but currently lives near the beach even though she hates sand. She's a full-time writer, time-waster extraordinaire, social media addict, coffee fiend, and ex-high school history teacher. She loves spending time with her two cats, alpha boyfriend, and chatting with readers. To learn more about Chelle, please visit her website.

JOIN MY VIP NEWSLETTER
chellebliss.com/newsletter

FOLLOW ME ON BOOKBUB
chellebliss.com/bb

Text Notifications (US only)
→ Text **GALLOS** to **24587**

Want to drop me a line?
authorchellebliss@gmail.com
www.chellebliss.com

Men of Inked: Southside Series

Maneuver - Book 1

Flow - Book 2

Hook - Book 3

Hustle - Book 4

MEN OF INKED SERIES

Throttle Me (FREE) - Book 1

Hook Me - Book 2

Resist Me - Book 3

Uncover Me - Book 4

Without Me - Book 5

Honor Me - Book 6

Worship Me - Book 7

Men of Inked Bonus Novellas

The Gallos (Bonus Book .5)

Resisting (Bonus Book 2.5)

Men of Inked Xmas (Bonus Book 6.5)

Rebound (Flash aka Sam)

ALFA INVESTIGATIONS SERIES

Sinful Intent - Book 1

Unlawful Desire - Book 2

Wicked Impulse - Book 3

ALFA Investigations Novellas

Rebound (Flash aka Sam)

Top Bottom Switch (Ret)

SINGLE READS

Mend

Enshrine

Misadventures of a City Girl

Misadventures with a Speed Demon

NAILED DOWN SERIES

Nailed Down - Book 1

Tied Down - Book 2

TAKEOVER DUET

Acquisition - Book 1

Merger - Book 2

FILTHY SERIES

Dirty Work

Dirty Secret

Dirty Defiance

LOVE AT LAST SERIES

Untangle Me - Book 1

Kayden the Past - Book 2

To learn more about Chelle's books visit *chellebliss.com*

ACKNOWLEDGMENTS

I should really start writing the acknowledgements as soon as I have the first words in any story. I always wait until the book is ready to publish and then remember every person who has played a role. Sounds like a solid plan, right? Wrong. It's an epic failure. By this point, my mind is practically useless and I'm rushing toward the finish line to press the publish button. But here I am. Again. Trying to remember every person who played a role to helping me create this book and I'm staring into the darkness, wishing I could even remember what I did yesterday.

So, lets try see how many people I can forget... again.

Lisa Hollett, Julie Deaton, and Rosa Sharon — ladies, you're a killer teach of editors and proofreaders. You're quick, kind, and always willing to dive right into my words. I know sometimes I sling a hot mess in your lap, but you never complain. I can't thank you enough for your hard work and support.

Lori Jackson — Thanks for an amazing original cover. I wish I could've used it and it'll show back up again. I swear. It's too beautiful not to be for sale. Your graphics are always spot on and totally beautiful.

Wendy Shatwell of Bare Naked Words — You're amazeballs. You totally put up with my crazy shit and never cuss me out. I don't know how you do it, but you have the patience of a saint.

Readers — What can I say? I'm a lucky son of a bitch for having an crazy fabulous group of readers who love my Gallo's. I don't know what I did to get so fucking lucky, but thank you for joining me on this crazy ride.

Betas and ARC readers — Ladies, you are hands down the best.

Brian — I know there are days I totally disappear as I chase a deadline. Thank you for always being understanding. I promise I'll get ahead someday. I swear. No really. It's all part of my plan.

Bliss Romance Hangout — You ladies (gentleman too) are always great at keeping my moral up and the words flowing. Any time I'm feeling down, just a quick stop into my fabulous reader group, and I'm right back on track. Thanks for loving my words.

I don't know who else I forgot. It's 5am and the

sun's not even out yet. I'm on my second cup of coffee, but my brain isn't functioning at maximum capacity just yet.

All I can say is thank you. Thank you to everyone. Without you I don't know where I'd be...

Made in the USA
Middletown, DE
11 October 2018